PHANTOM SIBLINGS

PHANTOM SIBLINGS

CAROLYN TAYLOR-WATTS

PUBLISHED IN 2021 BY
KINETICS DESIGN, KDBOOKS.CA

Copyright © 2021 by Carolyn Taylor-Watts

All rights reserved. No part of this publication may be reproduced or transmitted in any form or by any means, electronic or mechanical, including photocopying, recording, or any information storage and retrieval system, without permission in writing from the publisher.

Published in 2021 by
Kinetics Design, KDbooks.ca
ISBN 978-1-988360-48-5 (paperback)
ISBN 978-1-988360-49-2 (ebook)

Cover and interior design, typesetting, online publishing, and printing by Daniel Crack, Kinetics Design, KDbooks.ca
www.linkedin.com/in/kdbooks/

Contact the author at
www.carolyntaylorwatts.com

To Gordon Watts, my beloved husband,

who died before he could see this novel in print.

And to Michael Carroll for his very fine editing,

for believing in my story, for encouraging and supporting me

from the time of its genesis to its completion.

CHAPTER ONE

They say a person is driven to confess a crime, to tell someone what they've done before they die. Perhaps it's to boast. I was only in my mid-fifties and didn't plan to die anytime soon, but an urge to confess, to set right something in my past, had been creeping up on me. Then it hit me hard in the solar plexus.

It occurred the day after our New Year's Eve party in 2008 when Penny and I sat in idle conversation, each in our armchairs beside the window overlooking Vancouver's Coal Harbour. Mist floated up from the sea to blind our view of the harbour, so we turned and glanced at each other.

"What on earth happened to last year?" Penny asked. "Where did it go?"

Yes, where exactly? I found myself staring down the months, looking at another year the same as the last, the same as the one before that and before that, no new goal on the horizon, no new challenges — nothing to punctuate life's increasingly dull passage.

Surprised suddenly that I should have identified my life as dull, I drummed my fingers on the coffee table beside me, remembering a comment of this kind I'd made at one of our staff parties.

"It's because you don't have children to keep you on edge," a colleague had said. "Kids, you plan for things, then have to change them at the last minute. You've got to watch for stuff you hope will never happen, have eyes in the back of your head …"

"And dodge the bullets the little tyrants will fire at you," his wife had finished for him.

The reasons for Penny's and my childlessness were complicated. I didn't like to think about kids, or to have conversations about them, so now I slumped in my chair and watched the rain. I found myself making parallels between the seeming predictability of my life and the unswerving patterns of the raindrops … until that earlier conversation about children returned to disturb it.

Kids. Images of my young self slid across my mind like flashbacks in a movie. I knew that some people, as far back as high school or even before, had thought me a bit weird, a loner hovering on the fringes of things. Probably dull. But nobody knew — not even Penny — how deliberately I'd learned to mute my emotions. I was so successful that no one supposed me to have any. The reason I did was connected to my mom. Also to my Uncle Albert, but that, too, was a long story.

Dusk crept about the window, and I remained in the armchair, swallowed by shadows, until an overhead light was switched on and Penny, in her usual brisk voice asked, "Why are we sitting in the dark?"

"I'm meditating, thinking about the conversation some of us had a while ago about kids." At Penny's frown, I immediately added, "And also about my Uncle Albert."

"Oh? Has anything more about his estate come up?"

"No, it's not that."

"Oh." Penny lost interest, got up, and went into our bedroom where I heard her opening and closing drawers.

Freed for a further few minutes from what would have become a desultory verbal exchange, also to get my mind off kids, I deliberately conjured up Uncle Albert, my favourite person in the world. In my mind, his big face appeared furrowed with smiles. His light brown eyes, locked on mine, held particular warmth. Whenever he looked at me like that, I felt a sense of solidity, so for that day, for the next one, perhaps for a few into the future, I could relax, knowing my world was as stable and ordinary as everyone else's. When casting my mind back over my life, all those times he spent with me while I was in high school were the most comfortable and secure, the best parts of my childhood. Fragments of conversations now came to me.

"Come on, Julian, you've got a mathematical mind and a musical one, too. B grades aren't good enough."

"I, musical? How … how do you know?"

"Math and music often go together," he said. "Look at you — always drumming your fingers in time to rhythms and patterns only you can hear."

"Oh!"

Over the years, Uncle Albert had supported me in my love of music, encouraged me to study advanced math with the goal of attaining a degree in actuarial science, as he had. I'd stopped when I got as far as chartered accountancy. Enough of studying I felt, although I did truly enjoy math. Numbers were ordered and uncluttered and could be dealt with cleanly and then put away.

Still sunk in the armchair by the window, I closed my eyes, memories of Uncle Albert coming to me mixed up with previous conversations about children, mathematics, music. And so my thoughts clattered on. Raindrops kept falling. It occurred to me I might be bored with my job, even with my marriage. Whatever the cause, my present dissatisfaction troubled me because the truth was, in my life I had everything.

Gradually, I became aware of Penny moving around the kitchen. She must have floated noiselessly past my chair because I'd neither seen nor heard her. Now, wordlessly, she placed a glass of wine on the coffee table beside me. Pouring another, she settled herself in the swivel armchair opposite me and took up a book.

Marriage. Someone once said that if a man was married long enough, eventually his wife became his sister. My stomach twisted and I thought how totally unromantic that was. But when had I last contemplated love or romance? Then it came to me: in my heart, I craved intense emotion, something to crank up feelings of joy and wonder and sorrow. I'd experienced that once, but so long ago it might have been in another life. I glanced at Penny, her head bent over a novel, her feet on a stool. Did she feel my sense of inertia, of sliding disappointment, too?

Perhaps noticing that I was looking at her, she suggested out of the blue, "Why don't we throw a party to celebrate our thirtieth wedding anniversary?"

"That's a good idea. Yes, why not?" Surprised, pleased, I debated asking the reason for her sudden decision but feared it might take the edge off her obvious pleasure.

"We can show off our apartment to friends who haven't seen it," she continued, and warming to her own idea, immediately began an inspection of the eighteen hundred square feet of space we had on our building's fourteenth floor.

"Okay," I said. "I could invite a couple of old friends from Toronto I haven't seen in maybe more than twenty years."

"Jack, yes, ask him. And your cousin, Steve? What? Why are you looking like that?"

"I don't think so," I said quickly. At the mere mention of his name, images of my only cousin floated in my head, the last words he'd said to me resounding in my ears as guilt attacked me again.

"Okay, your decision," Penny said. "How about a

photographic display of both of us past and present? Give me the photos you've got."

For the next two weekends, she wandered around the living room, rubbing her hands, all sharp angles, efficient, matter-of-fact, as she planned and phoned, all the while muttering under her breath, "West Coast theme for food. Cheese trays. Fruit bowls. Finger food. Oh, yes, music, but not your kind, Jules. That'll be a bit too … intellectual. Flowers, streamers across the ceiling. Oh, and what about the invitation lists?"

Before the guests arrived the night of our anniversary party, I checked myself in the large mirror in the hallway. Not too different from the younger Julian Whitely, I persuaded myself, still with the square jaw, big ears, long, thin fingers — pianist's fingers, Uncle Albert had said — and a full but slightly crooked mouth.

Dissatisfied, uneasy even, I experienced the feelings I'd had as a teenager, that I'd been strung together by a collection of unrelated components and the different parts of me didn't properly hang together. A voice echoed out of the past, my father telling me in an uncharacteristic burst of praise, "My boy, the sum of your parts adds up to a damn good-looking fellow." But the mirror didn't support this optimistic view. The man reflected in it was of middling height and had a slight paunch, flat brown hair, and sun-spotted skin.

Dispirited by this cold analysis, I gazed at my wife to check how she had aged alongside me. Through the open door to our bedroom, I saw her seated before the dresser mirror examining herself, a makeup kit beside her. She looked up, her eyes following mine, over the lines crinkling her face, the groove between her brows, her thinning hair, the angular form of her fifty-nine-year-old body that in places stretched the fabric of her dress. An odd sensation of disappointment fell over me, and I rushed to hug her as though to silently apologize for my candid but ungenerous thoughts. She stood up to show off her dress, a light black-and-grey slippery thing that fell to her ankles in a sheer line. Penny was straight up and down like a tall poplar, I thought.

"No jewellery?" I asked.

"Jules, you know that's not me." She kissed my forehead lightly.

Later, during the party, unhappy with the physical appraisal of myself, I stood aside from our friends, mentally toting up a quick banker's calculation of the pluses and minuses of my life so that I could arrive at a sum: a comfortable condo on upscale Coal Harbour with a spectacular view over Burrard Inlet; beige carpeting, pale green walls on which hung etchings of musical instruments, bird motifs, two Norval Morrisseau paintings; a cherrywood table and chairs; an upright piano, above it, Giovanni Boldini's painting *The Woman in Red*.

The piano stood imperturbable with a rigid kind of grace. As our guests chatted in groups, my eyes lingered on its polished basswood, its warm ivory keys. A great urge to touch them swept over me, a desire to fill our living room with concertos and symphonies of the great masters of the past, not that I could ever do justice to them!

As I walked toward the piano, Penny hissed, "Not now, Jules. Not now." So to the background buzz of conversation I continued on with the calculations of my life: accountancy work on prestigious Howe Street, good friends, a happy marriage — all of it no small achievement for a piano tuner and accountant. But, to be sure, with the help of Uncle Albert.

Into this narration of my good fortune, that earlier sliver of dissatisfaction re-entered like a snake in a pristine garden. Solitary in the midst of all the revelry, I moved around in the kitchen lining up empty wine bottles, trying to decipher what I felt. I had almost finished stacking dirty dishes when a shout went up: "To Julian and Penny!" Voices boomed about the living room walls, and forgetting my momentary doubt, I rose up then, a king among friends, my wife a queen.

Sometime later, Penny's friend, Laura, stood before the photographic display on one of our living room walls and asked, "Hey, Julian, this was you?"

There, spread out like a graphic novel, hung my life and Penny's. As people crowded about, as Laura spoke about how personalities were sliced and judged, I thought how much we loved our pop psychology, our pseudo-Freudian interpretations of one another. A momentary sour feeling lodged in my throat.

Then Laura pointed a manicured finger at one of the snapshots. "This your mom and dad?"

I looked and cursed under my breath that I hadn't checked the photos Penny had pinned up. Bony, dishevelled, makeshift was the best brief description I could give of my dad. Beside him stooped my aproned mother, her hair lank, and I realized in surprise that she'd allowed herself to be photographed without her hair fussed with its usual perm. Dejection was etched in every bone in her body. I couldn't decode the background, so I had no idea where the picture had been taken.

"It wasn't a good day for him," I finally said, "or for my mother." I walked toward the darkened windows, recalling the time when I noticed a change in both my parents. Maybe I'd only registered it on reflection. I must have been about thirteen when the whisperings from my early childhood years resumed. Gathering in a crescendo, Mom moaned about the tribe of children she'd never had, and couldn't have. It made me, as her only child, feel it was my fault, that somehow I must make up for all her unborn and stillborn children.

While looking at the photos, I had a belated flash of insight. My mother had reached menopause and knew with finality she'd never have more. And so began the downward slide in her appearance, in her upkeep of our once immaculate house, eventually reaching the point in her and Dad's life captured in the snapshot Laura had pointed at. Or was it something else entirely?

Aware that I was now alone, I made a mental effort to re-enter my earlier jolly mood and joined Penny and her friends. They were back on the subject of mothers, children, schooling, play dates. Not that again. About to move away, I stopped, riveted by what Penny was saying.

"It's selfish to have children when there are so many orphans in the world who need good homes," she said.

Laura, who had to dominate every conversation, jumped in to point out how nature demanded perpetuation of the species. "Of course, we want children," she said, stocky body tilting forward, her expression earnest. "People love babies. Don't we all want to carry on our genes and, you know, become immortal?"

"I still say it's selfish," Penny insisted, her voice notably cooler.

I knew exactly what she was thinking, and suddenly there it was again: two people living together so long they'd begun to think the same, to finish each other's sentences, even to look alike, as some people said.

"It's an ego thing," Penny continued. "You just want little reproductions of yourself as though the world can't get enough of your perfect kind." But that last bit was uttered under her breath.

I turned away and spotted another group gathered around the piano — my piano. How I hated anyone else touching it except Penny, of course. Carrying my favourite drink of diet grapefruit juice and rum, I ambled back to the photographic display and stood before it, focusing on snapshots that showed our friends, our marriage, and my successful, though oddball, career. Any photo that suggested I was a misfit, a hippie when that era was over, I removed. I took down one or two others, as well, that revealed me as the kid always at the edge of others, stiff, awkward, unwanted-looking. Stuffing them in my suit jacket pocket, not caring if I crumpled them, I strode to the window to peer out over the sea and distant mountains. Pinpricks of light danced on the water, and while the whole scene was beautiful, right now my mind was unable to admire it.

Leaning against the window, I thought again about my young life. You'd think an only child would be coddled, prized, and spoiled. Not me. To Mom I was an ongoing source of hope, frustration, and disappointment. I'd felt the burden of it, had envied my friends their siblings, their tales of loves and hates and competition. I was jealous of their togetherness, their sharing, quarrels, and messiness. At home I felt alone, except when my cousin, Steve, was around. At school, and in the entire universe, I was straightened, trimmed, organized, and frowned over. No wonder I was stiff, awkward, and out of place. For the umpteenth time I wondered what Penny had ever seen in me.

"Julian." My wife's eyes were on me, one long, thin hand on my shoulder. "You look like you're on another planet. Come and join us around the piano. This is your big party."

"And yours," I said, recoiling as my colleague, Ian, started to enthusiastically bang away on the piano's keys. "Please don't do that!" I yelled at him.

Into the sudden silence, Penny stepped toward me and breathed in my ear, "Jules, he's our guest."

"I know and right now I don't care. No one has the right to do that to a piano."

Ian didn't hear me and continued thumping the keys. Our guests' voices shrilled with booze as they belted out "It's a Long Way to Tipperary."

Hunching my shoulders, I walked away, back to the photos, Penny following, begging me to be a good sport and not do anything to spoil the party.

"I'm sorry, honey," I whispered. "I'm just tired. I'm going to rearrange some of the photos because, well, there are some of me I wish we hadn't put up."

"Really? Which ones?" A shadow of annoyance clouded her eyes.

"This," I said, removing one in which my fifteen-year-old self lurked on the periphery of a group of gangly teenagers. It brought back the sliver of doubt I'd had earlier about my life, something important I'd forgotten, had lost, or had done. I couldn't for the life of me figure what it was.

"Don't be silly. Everyone has snapshots of themselves they don't like." Penny's voice was brusque. "They were in a shoebox in your cupboard. You saw me put them up and didn't complain. Anyway, just take a look around at your successful life." She put her hands on my shoulders and swivelled me about to see the faces of our revelling friends. Then she turned me back to the photos. "Jules, look at us together. We were happy then, weren't we?" It was a statement.

"We were indeed ... and aren't we now?"

"Of course, we are. I didn't mean that. It's just, well, I was so much better-looking back then."

She pointed to herself standing in the doorway of her apartment in a slim-line dress that fell from her shoulders to mid-calf, no breasts or hips to relieve its straight lines. Like a cloth covering a stick, I thought, and immediately felt surprise at this new image of my wife. Her pose was awkward, self-conscious, but she had squeezed out a smile for the camera. Then I thought, *Wow, this is new. Penny rarely reveals any vulnerability.*

"Not to me," I said. "You're even better-looking now." I

slipped an arm around her shoulders. "Just look at this one of you."

In the photo I indicated, Penny stood in baggy blue pajamas on our balcony, her feet apart, her hair tossed carelessly over her shoulders. It was the only time she'd worn her hair long, and I remembered that I'd wanted to capture that in a picture.

"You put *that* one up?" Penny frowned and reached out to remove the last snapshot. "It makes me look fat ..."

"*You* fat?" I laughed, but she ignored me.

"And to put it beside that bunch of girls. Sexy-looking classmates you had, Julian! Who's the one in the middle?"

I leaned forward for a better appraisal. A 1960s black-and-white picture showed a group of girls who all appeared much the same — except one. As I stared, a weird shock like a jolt of electricity coursed through me and my mouth went dry. Half hidden by her big hair, Louisa's merry eyes looked straight at me from across the years. Smothering an exclamation, I got closer, the better to see her cheeky smile, the come-hither look in her eyes, the nascent invitation in her body language. With Penny momentarily distracted by a guest, I ripped the photo off the wall. Before stuffing it in my jacket pocket, I examined it again, and shards of memory hit me so hard I dropped into a nearby chair. Louisa's eyes with their invitation had never been for me except for those few sweet years after I saved her twice from the school bully. And certainly never after what I'd done to her.

Louisa came into my life at the very end of my second year at Northern Secondary School in Toronto. She'd transferred from a school in Oakville, and I got only a glance here and there, a perfunctory smile, during those last few weeks of Grade 10. I wondered, as I allowed myself to remember her all these years later, whether she'd known I'd hung around just to look at her, to listen for her voice, to watch her with the other boys who jockeyed to be her date.

Now I understood the feeling of something missing when I'd been congratulating myself on my achievements. This girl, this sprite as I'd thought of her, must have been lurking deep in my brain, my pores, my every breath ever since I'd been a naive teenager. I'd forced her away from me, made her disappear down tunnels of time, stamped her out of sight and mind — until now. Damn the bloody photos!

"Julian!" The clamour for a speech had risen to a crescendo. Penny was studying me, annoyed, puzzled. Swallowing what remained of my drink, I glanced at the flushed faces of our friends but avoided Penny's eyes. Lights from the harbour blinked through the open windows. Someone crashed a chord on the piano as though to command silence, and I muffled my shout not to do that, walked to the piano, and ignoring Ian's surprised expression, closed the lid.

"Julian," Penny whispered, "what are you doing?"

"Sorry," I muttered. "That's my baby and I won't have anyone — *anyone* — banging on it." Forcing myself to recall the earlier tally of my successes, I gazed at the expectant faces staring at me, struggling to remember the speech I'd rehearsed.

Penny's breath was in my ear. "It's our party, Julian. You have to make a speech. I saw you writing one."

When finally I began, when I got to the part where I mentioned Northern Secondary, suddenly, unbelievably, the face I'd seen in the photo smacked right up against mine and breathed hotly on me. "What the devil? Get out of my face!" But the words weren't mine — or maybe they were — and fraught silence hung in the room.

"He saw someone in the photos we posted, someone who hurt him," Penny said, a flush staining her cheeks.

Louisa's laughing face assailed me, together with a bolt

of something cold and hard that shot through me. Many hands reached out as I stumbled. Too much to drink, they'd think, but I knew what it was. Rubbing my face, blinking, I opened my mouth to say something, but nothing came out. My heart pounded with the violence of excitement, of fear, maybe both. It was at that moment I knew I had to go back in time and fix what I'd done. And it wasn't just about the need to confess.

Deep in the chair where many hands lowered me, I dropped my spinning head to my chest and closed my eyes. While anxious voices punctuated the air around me, I remained sunk, waiting for the flapping figures to be gone, for the party to be over.

After the last guest left, Penny drifted around the living room, picking up a dirty glass here and there, paper napkins from the floor. She was avoiding me, and any mention of how I'd behaved. Generally, she faced issues head-on, but this was something she didn't know how to deal with; she needed more information and knew it might take time to get it. I saw her lips settle in a straight white line, the contours of her face sharpen. This, or I should say I, had become a problem that must be broken into components, each one analyzed, then fixed.

Eventually abandoning her half-hearted cleaning, Penny stepped to the piano, lifted the lid, and ran her fingers over the keys. A Chopin waltz softly filled the air and briefly soothed my restless brain. Time slipped away. I had no idea how many hours passed, or what I did with them, only becoming aware of a vague feeling of emptiness. Opening my eyes, I searched about, noting the absence of any colour — the walls, the floor, the view out the window. Penny wasn't anywhere. Pulling myself out of the chair, I staggered into our bedroom, hung up my jacket, folded my clothes, and put them on a chair, my shoes on my side of the walk-in closet.

This was the order of things done in our house. Only then did I fall into bed in an exhausted slumber.

Sometime later Penny slipped in beside me. In the creaking silence of the early hours, I awoke and looked at her: the sagging face, faded hair straggling across the pillow, the long, thin form that stretched across more than half the bed.

"Julian?"

"Ugh ... what ... what?" But it was Louisa's face close to mine, Louisa's hooded eyes holding bitterness that stared at me. Wide awake now, I remembered from the previous night that there was something I had to do. With a frantic sense of time running out, not to make amends for what I'd done to Louisa but to remove all memory of it, of her, I got up. Fumbling with my dressing gown and slippers, I went to the living room, hell-bent on finding and ripping up any snapshots of Louisa that might remain in the shoebox Penny had discovered on the bottom bookcase shelf. Maybe then she would be gone, dead, a girl I'd loved with all the passion of my young and lonely heart, a girl I'd sent away after telling her I didn't love her and never had. *I love yet am forced to seem to hate ...* Who had said that?

First, I retrieved the crumpled photo from my blazer pocket and tore it up. *Don't look at it!* Next, I searched for any photos of Louisa. There were only two of her standing in the middle of a group of teenagers — how could I have missed them? I shredded them and dropped the pieces onto the floor. Chilled but sweaty in a cold night breeze that blew through the open window, I watched the sky darken beyond the harbour, lighten, then darken again as a rising moon scudded across the waters of Coal Harbour. It was a shifting light that reflected my mood. When dawn crept about the window, still I hunched in a living room chair, a few photos scattered in my lap and on the floor. How I longed for the joy that memories could bring, yet didn't. How I hungered to experience again the sweet, compelling, world-altering emotions I'd held for a girl called Louisa, a girl who had been the very reason for my existence, who had awakened my long-shuttered emotions. The recollection terrified me. I knew it could engulf my life, even now after all the decades that had passed. I had to push her back into a dark tunnel and block it up, never think of her again. The moment I decided this, the yearning for that great emotion washed over me again. Just one succulent taste of it, I thought. Why had I looked at the photos? To punish myself? Because of a momentary self-destructive impulse? Maybe guilt that had to be explained and atoned for?

The early-morning sun lit remnants of last night's party: red-stained wineglasses; dirty bowls and plates piled on top of the dishwasher; cards, paper wrapping, food scraps, cushions on the floor. I bent to pick up the scattered photos I'd ripped up. I wouldn't look, but I did. One fragment revealed Louisa silhouetted against the fractured light of a wide sky kissing the lake at a beach in Toronto, and there it was: the cheeky half-smile, the come-hither expression in eyes that gazed boldly into mine.

Motionless, I stared at the photo, then angrily stuffed it in my dressing gown pocket. Sweeping up pieces of other pictures, I threw them into a plastic bag, tied it up, and put it in the recycling box.

Several nights later while I was taking down the rest of the photographic display, another face jumped into mine: a shot of Steve and me, my cousin's eyes brimming with triumph. The two of us were wildly laughing, our foreheads almost touching, freckles burning under the hot summer sun. Steve had probably just beaten me in a game of tennis, soccer, or baseball, as he always did. I never really cared.

Steve — anger, and a sense of loss fell over me. The two of us had been polar opposites, but as kids had played together on weekends and during whole summers. In games of hide-and-seek, we flitted through the cemetery — Steve lived on its southern edge on Toronto's Moore Avenue. We yelled and chased each other, jumping over headstones until Mom raised an upstairs window and yelled, "Stop that! You're committing blasphemy!"

I remembered how Steve always had to win at everything. When he didn't — a rare occasion — a cold expression settled in his eyes, like two stones at the bottom of a river. In those days, we walked together to Northern Secondary, sat together for classes, until I got high grades and Steve fell near the bottom. It was then that our relationship began to change.

"You're being very odd, Julian." I jumped in my chair as Penny's voice cut through my musings. "Ever since our anniversary party, I hardly know you anymore. Can't you deal with whatever it is?" It was a Sunday, eight days after our celebration. Penny was in her dressing gown, hair tied carelessly in a ponytail, leafing through the *Vancouver Sun*.

Her comments were so like her: get hold of yourself, pull yourself together.

But strange waking dreams continued to plague me, and restless, I paced about the apartment, went to work, came home, and went out again. I never touched the piano. At times I felt drugged, half awake, half asleep. Penny's light brown eyes rested unhappily on mine, on my tired face and bloodshot eyes. She opened her mouth to say something, then closed it again. We ate dinners she prepared in silence. Over the weeks, she started putting a magazine beside her plate and pretended to read it. Afterward I cleaned up, walked to the window, folded my arms, and stared out at the evening. Penny spread out school papers or report cards on the dining room table or took a book and went to our bedroom to read.

Before bed one night, I remembered the fragment of

photo I'd stuffed in my dressing gown pocket. Pulling it out, I studied it until time wound itself backward. As shadows crept over the North Shore Mountains, I locked myself in a cage of memories, tumbled back through a hole in time when I didn't belong to myself.

CHAPTER TWO

Hurrah for the 1960s! Hurrah for the Beatles! For no reason at all, I jumped out of bed that cool October morning and set the needle on a vinyl record, turning up the sound to hear Lennon and McCartney's "Yellow Submarine," with Ringo on the vocals. There was time to play it before I went to school. Or so I thought, when Mom's voice shouted up the stairs, "Shut that thing off, will you?"

Damn, I'd forgotten it was one of my dead sibling's birthdays — it had to be Jeremy's. He'd died before I was born and lived only one month — a crib death, the doctor had called it. I skipped the record to "Nowhere Man," more appropriate to the mood that would lurk in our house all day. I'd come home after school to it all, too: Mom on my case to be respectful, to be quiet, to turn off my music, and especially not to play the Beatles. "You don't want to desecrate the memory of your brother, poor angel, do you?" she'd say. I was so used to her moods and behaviour, which by anyone's standards would seem extremely odd, that I saw it as sort of normal. Except for a comment like this, it was understood in our family that we wouldn't mention Mom's phantom babies. Once or twice when I was younger, I was tempted to ask why they remained babies and didn't become toddlers — little kids — in other words, why they didn't grow up. Intuitively, I understood I could never ask that.

Leaving for school early, I took up my usual post by the

ragged pine tree near the main entrance, listening to voices: to the kids around me, and kids from the past; the sound of feet that walked, hopped, ran, and skipped to this place since 1930 when the school first opened. My friends, Jack and Robbie, typically slid through the doors at the last minute, so I wouldn't see them until first break. There was no sign of Steve.

Nothing I did drowned out Mom's whisperings. A birthday always got her going about her missing children, and she cursed God, fate, and her husband that she'd managed only one — me, a tall, lanky boy with a big head, big ears and hands, a boy who made no sports teams, no debating clubs, who had few friends and couldn't even stand up to bullies. On days I arrived home from school bruised and bloodied, she assumed an expression of shame that also held accusation. Under her breath she muttered, "That boy has never given me anything to be proud of, and heaven knows how I've tried. Clueless, that's what he is." I would give her a fleeting look to check out how bad the afternoon and evening were going to be. Usually, if her face was doughy and so scrunched up that her eyes all but disappeared, I'd tell her I had to be at Jack's or Robbie's for homework, then skedaddle out of there.

We lived on Merton Street between Mount Pleasant Road and Bayview Avenue in Toronto. Our house was like many others — the typical 1940s square box with living room, dining room, a kitchen and a sunroom off it, three bedrooms upstairs. Mom and Dad had the big one facing the street. Mine was one of the two smaller ones at the back overlooking the cemetery. The third was shared by two of my three dead siblings, Genevieve and Susannah. For Jeremy, Mom had made a tiny bedroom at the end of the hallway, put a cot in it, a small white chest of drawers, and a curtain to close it off. I especially dreaded going past my sisters' room if the door was open because it creeped me out. Tiny cries might come from the walls, the floor, the ceiling. Mostly, I dreaded it because of an enlarged photograph of Genevieve hanging above her bed. She had been five months old when it had been taken. Her image haunted me: wide blue eyes where shadows lurked, a tiny mouth puckered in a half-smile, half-grimace, both fists tightly balled. I wondered if she had intuited she was about to slip away.

There was a long, narrow back garden that ended at a wooden fence separating us from the north end of Mount Pleasant Cemetery. I recalled once asking Dad if Mom's dead babies were buried there, just over the wall. The two of us had been working in the basement, Dad building a birdhouse while I hammered and sawed at planks that I hoped would one day resemble a floating raft. A companionable silence stretched between us, and I supposed that was why I'd had the nerve to come straight out and ask, "Dad, about Mom's pretend babies …"

"Damn!" Dad swore as his hammer came down on his thumb. Without looking at me, he said in a flat voice, "It's best not to talk about any of that."

Mom's pretend babies. And Steve's voice from our childhood floated back to me, together with images of the two of us playing in the cemetery. I'd just explained to him that when I heard sounds, I saw them as colours. He glanced at me sideways and said, "I never heard anything like that." Then, without looking at me, added, "They say your Mom's a bit … funny. I've heard whispers about her dead babies. You, Julio, you better be careful you don't go that way, too."

I wondered whether the buying of our house right up against the cemetery was deliberately done to cater to Mom's delusions, or simply a good and affordable place to live. How could my dead baby brother and two sisters be buried over there, but at the same time still be alive upstairs in their bedrooms? All my young life I brooded on it. I wanted to ask, didn't know how, and implicitly understood that such questions were taboo.

To other people it would be bizarre that my mother pretended her missing children were still alive and she furnished bedrooms for them. That she talked to them, sang them nursery rhymes. That she made them clothes and celebrated their birthdays with iced cakes. Jeremy, as I said, lived for a month, Susannah was stillborn, and Genevieve survived until she was almost six months.

As a small boy, I took my cues from Dad to glean clues how I should act around Mom, especially those times when she locked herself in her bedroom or sat on the babies' beds all weekend, singing to them, reading stories to them. When things were really bad, I noticed Dad avoided looking directly at me, but I saw that his eyes were flat, the light emptied out of them. Like the time he found her lying on the frozen grass in our backyard in the middle of January and had her taken to the hospital. On another occasion, a neighbour found her in her dressing gown sitting on the concrete steps of Mount Pleasant Baptist Church and brought her back. That time, the minute Dad got home from work he called our family doctor, who came to the house and sedated her. The doctor dropped in a few times after that, and maybe a week or two later, declared she was improving and could get up and about, could go for outings.

She would be okay for a few months and then begin a slow slide backward, spending more time in the babies' bedrooms. Through my closed door, I heard her weeping or singing nursery rhymes. It could go on for days. Eventually, Dad managed to get her into the car and take her to the doctor. Mostly, I could block out her behaviour, or I got so used to it that I didn't see it as totally weird as other people would — if only they knew! I supposed the neighbours on each side of us had an idea, but never spoke of it. Also, Mom was still sufficiently tuned in to ordinary life that she gave few clues about what went on in our house, not even to her friends. But then she and Dad didn't have many. I mean, it was rare for them to invite people in. Usually, if they wanted to entertain or to celebrate a family occasion, they'd invite them to a restaurant.

When it came to family members, we didn't really have many. There was Dad's brother, Uncle Albert, whose wife had died long ago. And Dad's other brother, Uncle Robert; his wife, Aunt Lindy; and his son, Steve. We saw Aunt Lindy and Uncle Robert once or twice a year, and my aunt not always then. Steve, on the other hand, was a mystery. In our teenage years, Mom discouraged my relationship with him, and when Steve once suggested he and I go off together some evenings, she bluntly refused to let me.

"Too much homework," she'd say without looking at me. "Too many responsibilities."

"Why don't you like him? What's he done?"

"Don't ask me. I'm sure I don't know," she'd say as she flipped the pages of a recipe book on the kitchen counter.

My only cousin. Whenever our paths crossed in our later teenage years, he acted as a know-it-all wiseass. He laughed at me for being ignorant, a weirdo. One particular Christmas at our house he sidled up to me. "Hey, kiddo," he said, "listen up and I'll let you in on something." He pulled me into the little sunroom at the back of the kitchen and thrust himself close to me, invading what I called my body buffer zone, challenging me. But about what? His eyes, often the colour of weeds in dirty pond water, flared like two grey-brown pebbles. "You're what, sixteen, seventeen?" he asked. "Old enough. Hang around with me some time and get yourself out from under Uncle Albert. Maybe you're his pet of the moment —" my cousin's mouth twisted "— but he'll get tired of you soon enough."

I cringed as Uncle Albert's name came out as a sneer.

"So," he said, edging still closer to me, "I'm asking, do you want to run with the big boys?"

Through the open kitchen doorway, I could see into the living room, to Uncle Albert leaning against the fireplace mantel, listening to Mom's little transistor radio, his long, slim fingers tapping out a rhythm on the mantel shelf. Dad stood beside him, and he, too, began rapping in time to the beat.

Mom was at the living room window with Aunt Lindy, pointing at the front garden, chattering about the summer past. I caught snippets about the best yellow gladiola blooms she'd ever had, the best blue irises. I exhaled a large breath. She was acting *normal*. Forgetting Steve who was waiting impatiently for my answer, I started worrying about the babies upstairs. Would Mom suddenly remember them, rush up there, play lullabies, and cry? Would she become weird? I stopped my thoughts, tried to concentrate on the here and now, on these ordinary family moments.

Steve lifted his shoulders, flexed his bulky forearms. "Lost your tongue?" The sneer was still there in his voice.

"Ugh, um, I don't know. Can we talk about this some other time? Let's just enjoy Christmas." I turned away, not seeing contempt enter his eyes, not aware of his withdrawal from me, from the whole Christmas party, that this would be the last time he'd invite me into his world, whatever that was.

As we sat down to dinner, "White Christmas" played softly in the background. Forgetting Steve, who sat like a hulk at one end of the table, I considered this was the best Christmas I could remember. Family. Music. The aromas of roasted turkey with all its accompaniments. Steam rising through the white chrysanthemums in the centre of the table as Mom leaned over it and smiled. The table, the room, the whole house spangled. I looked again at Mom. She was still smiling, but the slimness of her shadow grabbed at my heart. I wanted to touch her, tell her I loved her, let her know everything would always be okay. But I didn't move. I said nothing. That was the way in our house.

Uncle Albert smiled down the table at me, his fingers resting on it, shoulders straight. Warmth, like the embers of a fire, emanated from him. Uncle Robert sat beside him in a sort of crouched position, eyes shifting rapidly from one family member to the other. They were brothers, yes. Same parents, same background, but how to explain the enormous differences?

Uncle Albert winked at me. Steve saw it. Uncle Robert, too. Then Uncle Robert's oily voice cut through the air. "Julian, have you made any sports teams at school?"

I shook my head, mouth full of turkey.

"No good at sports, eh? Don't play any? Steve, tell your cousin how you helped win the intercollegiate soccer trophy for your high school. Tell him about that great final kick, that you're the school's big hero and everyone's still talking about it."

"But wasn't that last year?" Mom asked Steve. "I thought you left school. What *are* you doing with yourself now?" Her voice was pretty, normal. But my wave of happiness at noting that got cut off by the silence that descended on the table. Aunt Lindy bowed her head as though in prayer, her curly greyish-brown hair falling over her face to hide it. Steve cracked his knuckles and stared at his plate. Uncle Robert made fists and glared at everyone.

Into that silence, I raised my voice. "Okay, listen. Steve was the best soccer player in the whole school and was on the tennis team, too. He's a great sportsman."

"So Steve really did leave school?" Mom murmured in wonder. "I didn't believe it when somebody told me."

Steve's expression said, "As if you would care," but his fleeting glance at me held gratitude.

"Steve's following in his father's footsteps," Uncle Robert said, and I saw from the sound of his voice, the colour of creosote. "A son working with his father. Remember I said just a month ago, Muriel, how I need an assistant in my printing business because it's expanding every year — three shops now — and who else but my boy? He'll do great things."

"*Aghh!*" Steve was on his feet, eyes popping. "You call that a business? I never worked there and never will. It's a dirty business. Nothing but a hole of a place. Keep it for some other sucker — ha, maybe for you, dear cousin Julian. What are *you* going to do with yourself when *you* leave school?"

With a violent motion, he pushed back his chair. Behind the rage in his eyes I detected sadness. Dumbly, I watched as he stumbled suddenly, clutching the edge of the table.

"Watch it!" Mom cried out as the table tilted. *"Oh, no, no, no, no!"*

"Stop it!" I yelled as I leaped up, and Steve jumped, too. My longing for this to be a normal Christmas almost choked me, and my first impulse was to let Steve have it for destroying it. The dishes were sliding, first the cauliflower casserole, then the gravy dish, the roasted potatoes …

"Grab it!" yelled Dad, reaching across the table to catch the thirty-pound roast turkey in its stainless-steel dish.

In the aftermath of the chaos, after the part of the dinner retrieved had been consumed, Steve approached me again, only now with a trace of wistfulness in his voice. We were back in the sunroom, Steve extracting a cigarette from his jacket pocket and lighting it. "Last chance. Want one of these?" He extended the pack to me. I shook my head. "Want to do something after school with the big boys?"

"I … I don't know. Maybe some … other time …" My voice trailed away as I tried to imagine what big boys did.

Steve's expression reduced me to nothing, and suddenly I felt as insignificant as Mom's phantom babies were to the world. A fleeting thought crossed my mind, that Steve was jealous of Uncle Albert's attention to me. But why had he dropped out of school at age sixteen? What was he doing now? Nobody seemed to know. I couldn't imagine him working in one of his father's print shops. He was too restless and needed an outdoors kind of job.

His eyes upon me had returned to cold little stones, and he flicked his thick black hair off his forehead. I saw him glance through the kitchen door at Mom collecting dirty plates from the table, Aunt Lindy brushing crumbs off the tablecloth, at the two men standing before the fireplace, Uncle Robert with a beer, Dad with a glass of red wine. In my mind, Steve rose up off the carpet above us all, knowing, cunning, manipulative. But there had also been that flicker of sadness in his eyes.

"I can twist my mom and dad to get whatever I want," he said now. But the words came out as those of a little boy, and there he was, dropped back to earth, his feet on the pale blue-grey carpet of the living room.

"Well, what *do* you want?" I asked.

"Unless you become one of the big boys, you'll never know, kiddo." He shrugged and blew a puff of smoke in my face.

Kiddo? While I stood a foot taller than him, while I knew I could best him in a fight, there was something vaguely menacing about him. Again, there was the sadness I'd seen behind his eyes. Nothing about him computed.

All through that January, dull and without snow, as I rode my bike through the cemetery delivering newspapers in the mornings, flyers in the evenings after dinner, sometimes I thought I saw Steve in the distance, around a shop corner, through the trees in the cemetery, or behind the shadows cast by headstones. His figure was distinctive: boxy shoulders, short neck with the head crunched low on it. But the ghostly form never quite revealed itself. Maybe I imagined him.

"Have you heard anything from Steve, or Uncle Robert, for that matter?" I asked Dad that evening, still spooked by my cousin's phantom presence. Dad looked up from his newspaper and mumbled something about Uncle Robert being out of the country. Mom turned up her little radio as though not wanting to hear.

"What about Steve?"

"After he dropped out of school," Dad said finally, "we thought he went to work in one of his father's print shops. But it seems that never happened. I wouldn't worry about him, though."

"I'm not *worried*."

CHAPTER THREE

Back when I was about nine, Uncle Albert dropped over and said he would take me for baseball practice. Mom, in the middle of waxing the dining room table, turned and rolled her eyes. "It's good of you, Albert, but you're wasting your time. Julian's no good at sports."

I heard this from the back porch and knew Mom hadn't intended to be mean. I was supposed to make up for all the kids she never had, couldn't have, or had lost. Even at a young age, I knew I disappointed her in every way imaginable. She'd seen me once on Davisville Park's baseball diamond and on the tennis courts, so she knew. She'd given up. This after trying hard to create the boy she wanted, after giving me baseball bats, softballs, tennis racquets, skates, and skis for birthdays and Christmases. All the sports equipment lay dust-covered in our garage.

Uncle Albert did take me to Davisville Park and threw balls at me on the baseball diamond. Then we moved to the tennis courts. Afterward, he said to Mom, "Muriel, your boy has no large-muscle coordination. He can't hit the ball and can't catch it. He doesn't want to play baseball and, in fact, doesn't like team sports."

A tense silence followed. "Well, what a surprise," Mom said as she wiped her hands on a tea towel. "He's exactly like you. Two peas in a pod."

Uncle Albert stared at her, but when he spoke, his voice was low-key, the colour of a dewy dawn, I thought. "What

Julian wants to do is learn to play a musical instrument, like the piano. Hasn't he told you how he's learning to read music at school with the help of the music teacher?"

Mom shook her head and glared at me reproachfully.

"Jules, you should share these things with your mother. She likes to keep up with what you're doing." Turning back to my mom, Uncle Albert said, "So instead of all the sports stuff, why don't we set him up with formal piano lessons? He's good at math, too, and everyone knows music and math go together. If you're good at one, you're usually good at the other, or you could be if you're given the chance."

"Oh ..." A look of relief fell over Mom's face, relaxing the taut lines around her mouth.

Uncle Albert was just warming up to his subject. "So much is embodied in mathematical expressions." A distant expression settled over his face. "You played the piano once, Muriel. You might remember how time signatures, rhythm and harmony, intervals, patterns, all the notations and sounds of the composers, are connected to mathematics. So, about your boy." He turned back to me, eyes boring into mine. "Julian, the next time you hear classical or operatic music, or rock, folk, jazz, or pop, for that matter, just think what math and music have in common. Think how together they're used to create every kind of music. But back to math. To be clever isn't enough. You have to work at it hours every day, unless you're a savant, and that you're not. Are you up for it?"

I rocked back and forth on my feet and clasped my hands. Blood tingled hotly inside me. "Up for piano lessons, yes siree! But —" my voice dropped suddenly "— we don't have a piano for me to practise on."

"I wouldn't worry about that for the moment," he said, winking.

Uncle Albert turned his attention to Mom, but I didn't listen further because my mind had slipped past the talk about music and back to the comment Mom had made: *He's exactly like you. Two peas in a pod.* I leaned against the living room mantel, feeling pleased, proud, and somehow more important, until Mom's voice penetrated.

"Where exactly are we to get the money to buy a piano for him to practise on, or for lessons, for that matter?" Her voice was fretful. "Who's going to pay for it all?"

Uncle Albert didn't answer for a moment but stood and cocked his ear. "What's going on upstairs?"

I knew what it was, and was so familiar with it that I barely heard it anymore. My jaw tightened, and I couldn't look at Mom. How on earth was she going to explain? Also, how could Uncle Albert not know?

Mom's face went pink, and she shook her head. Before she turned her back on him, I saw a mask-like expression fall over her face, the one she assumed when embarrassed. She went into the dining room quickly, slippers slapping on the polished floor. From the table she picked up the placemat she was crocheting, sat down with it in her swivel armchair, and acted as if we weren't there.

"Lullabies," I said into the empty air. Then, unable to stop myself, I added, "I guess one of her dead babies is having a birthday."

"What the devil!" Uncle Albert listened for a bit longer, staring up the stairs.

I could see Mom through the doorway to the dining room, saw her hunch her shoulders further, still with her back to us. Then she put down her needlework and pretended to fix her hair, pinning up stray bits and tying them into a bun.

Uncle Albert's eyes were focused on her back, wide and disbelieving. "Have you gone mad — or what?" His voice boomed around the kitchen and into the dining room, loud and angry. "Look at me when I'm talking to you, Muriel! You … you were always so … oh, what the hell! I thought you'd got over all that. Look, you've got one live kid, haven't you? For God's sake, look after *him* instead of all your phantom ones." He made to step out the side door, only to swing back. "Really, don't you think you should go back and see that doctor?" Not waiting for her to answer, he strode through the door and down the steps without another word or a glance at either of us.

Mom's face had darkened to a furious red. Her eyes popped wide, and she yelled at me, "You, you're no good for anything! How dare you let out family secrets to the world!"

"Uncle Albert isn't the world," I said sulkily. "He's Dad's brother. Anyway, I thought he already knew." Then I remembered a question that long ago I'd wanted to ask and never had for fear of the reaction I'd get. This seemed the right time, and I summoned up the courage. "Does Uncle Robert know about the babies?" I figured he did because of what Steve had said, but wanted to test her out. "And is that the reason he and Aunt Lindy don't visit us much anymore?"

"Uncle Robert?" Mom seemed confused for a moment. "Oh, him." She waved a hand in the air in dismissal, and I learned nothing further. Another question for Uncle Albert.

Mom remained with her shoulders hunched, head bowed over her sewing. She had put aside her crocheting and begun stitching what looked like a tiny jacket — some cute piece of clothing for one of her dead kids, I thought sourly.

Even as a boy, a young teenager, I saw in general that Mom was a disappointed woman — also cold, exacting, and obsessive. The house must be tidy, nothing out of place, things put away the minute they were used, never was there an end to how everything must be done. But I also saw how pure was the expression of pleasure on her face when she opened the linen cupboard and gazed at her lavender perfumed, perfectly folded towels, sheets, and pillowcases.

I never got any such expression, not even close.

CHAPTER FOUR

One early Saturday afternoon I was in the living room moving pieces around a chessboard. On the soundtrack, quietly, I played Paul and Linda McCartney's song "Uncle Albert/Admiral Halsey." My mind was full of my Uncle Albert then, especially the way he'd walked out of our house that last time. I felt partly responsible because I'd been the one to bring up the subject of the dead babies.

The song was a strange one perhaps, but it was appropriate for our house. It was made up of several unfinished song fragments that McCartney stitched together, similar to the medleys from the Beatles' *Abbey Road* album. I played it often because of its sound effects — the noise of thunderstorms and rain, squawking seabirds, wind by a seashore. I knew, too, that McCartney's "Uncle Albert/Admiral Halsey" was based on his uncle, someone he was very fond of. I believed he also used it as a form of apology from his generation to the older one. To me, the Uncle Albert section of the song revealed McCartney's emotions in the aftermath of the breakup of the Beatles, his personal apology for his, and his generation's, lethargy. Like being easily distracted, getting nothing done, and even for being depressed.

It occurred to me by playing the song I might subconsciously be apologizing to Mom for my attitude, for not having enough compassion for her, for not being the kind of son she longed for. Putting aside the chessboard, I sat back and concentrated on the song's words, on the colours the sounds created: light and dark pinks interspersed with streaks of smoky blues. Outside on the street, kids laughed and kicked around a soccer ball.

I figured Mom knew I was in there, but she never said a word as she made preparations for dinner. When Dad came home, she looked up from whatever she was cooking. He stepped forward to give her a peck on the cheek. She turned her face away, and in a loud voice said, "*You* do something with that boy! He's no good at anything! He doesn't even try to —" Her voice held the echo of tears. "Tell me, why isn't he out there with the other kids on the street doing what ordinary kids do?"

I badly wanted to say, *How can I be an ordinary kid with a mother like you? You should look at yourself. Nothing is ordinary in this house.* Of course, I never did say such things because I'd learned long ago to smother my feelings. I would achieve nothing, anyway.

"Now just a minute, Muriel." Dad, business-like in his pressed grey trousers and maroon blazer, moved back to the kitchen door to stand framed in its doorway. The six o'clock traffic buzzed behind him along Merton Street, and above it faintly, I heard the shouts of kids still playing on the sidewalk. Dad's normally placid voice interrupted what I knew would otherwise have become a tirade from Mom. His gentle blue-grey eyes settled on me through the living room doorway. "Julian's no ordinary kid. He's special."

He walked into the room, looked at the pieces on the chessboard, lifted my chin in his big hands, and when he spoke again, I heard in his voice colours in the blue-grey spectrum: pale blues, mauves, and soft greys. "It looks like you stood up to those bullies pretty well. Good lad." At this approval I thought nothing of the remnants of the bleeding neck and hands I'd come into the house with and had mostly cleaned up.

Dad remained motionless for a moment or two more, glancing at Mom, then at me, and back to Mom. He must have decided to press his case on my behalf because he straightened his shoulders. Enunciating forcefully, he said, "Muriel, your son does well at school. He gets high marks in math and music. He's also clever with his hands — a remarkable skill he's got. Why don't you take a look at the miniature instruments he's sculpted in the basement? They're extraordinary. This is what he wants to do — build things. I bet you didn't know that he's got dreams of one day building a piano. Why don't you tell him just once that you're proud of him?"

"Obviously because you've already been telling him." Mom picked up a saucepan lid and slammed it on a pot on the stove. "Besides," she said, "he never tells me anything." She kept her head down as she stirred whatever was in a second pot. "As for dreaming," she added, "the boy can certainly do that." She made a noise of disgust.

You're talking about me as though I'm not here, I thought, anger bubbling inside me. "The boy?" I said out loud. "I do have a name, you know."

"Yes — *Julian*." Mom raised her head, glanced from me to Dad and back to me. "In the balance of things, I'd say you're altogether your father's son."

This was a complicated statement. Physically, I wasn't much like my dad, significant only because of my gawky height and ears that stuck out, my head always cocked to one side as though listening for something no one else could hear. But I shared some of his interests, like woodworking, making things, wanting to know how stuff operated. I knew Mom thought I'd end up like him, and aside from his job with the Clarkson Gordon accounting firm, like him, I'd spend my life tinkering with tools and machinery. Mentally, I was sharper than Dad, and she knew it. I also knew she'd give anything to be able to say something like this: "My son, Julian, the doctor, the cardiologist. My son, the prosecutor, the judge, the bank manager." But all she could say at the moment was: "My son, Julian, who wants to be a piano tuner."

∞

July 4 was the birthday of my dead sibling, Genevieve. I came out of my bedroom at about seven, and there was Mom leaning against Genevieve's door frame, twisting a tissue in her hands. Her white dressing gown with the lavender flowers embroidered on it flapped around her legs, and her hair was loose. The dressing gown had been Dad's gift to her at the birth of Genevieve. At home she wore it most of the time as though it would help maintain her belief that her baby was still alive. I glimpsed a cavernous darkness under her eyes and quickly looked away.

She saw me sneaking a peek at her and turned her tear-stained face away. After a few moments, she asked in a cold, accusing voice, "Why can't you aspire to more? Tinkering, that's all you do. Surely, you can go farther than your Uncle Albert. I mean, must you really model yourself on him?" She spun away, slumping until she resembled a crumpled ball. Holding on to the railing, she clumped down the stairs and into the kitchen.

I felt an urgent need for Uncle Albert and his solace, so I summoned my last image of him. We were in his apartment at St. Clair and Walmer Road — how I loved that place! It was so full of him: music sheets scattered over his piano and on the floor, Impressionist prints, glass sculptures, walls of shelves holding an eclectic collection of books. On that visit he leaned against his upright piano dressed in a blazer and pressed jeans. His hair straggled over his large brow and his eyes beneath it were soft, warm, as though to invite confidences. The colours surrounding him were orange, yellow, a soft mauve. Then he leaned over me, painstakingly telling me about the history of the piano, impressing on me the unique instrument it was, how complex with more than fifty parts for each key and more than seven thousand total parts for a grand piano.

"This instrument," he said, face bent near mine, "this piano here, it's the culmination, the perfection, of all the stringed instruments. Look, why don't I teach you a few chords right now? Come on, let's sit down."

Next thing he was on the stool beside me, his fingers softly stroking the keys. Colours flew in the air as he struck the major chords, and I laughed as a sort of ecstasy filled me. My feelings were so intense and unfamiliar that they scared me. It was as though someone else inhabited me.

I left his apartment that day, smiling, laughing, punching the air — indestructible.

Afterward, as I wandered out to Mount Pleasant Road, my mind drifted to another conversation with him. In formal tones I guessed he used for teaching students, he'd said, "Julian, it takes amazing physical, intellectual, and emotional brilliance to play such a complex instrument as a piano in a truly captivating way. You know what I think? That only a tiny proportion of the world's pianists are up to the job. Do you think you are? Are you willing to put in the time and become one of those?"

Pumped, proud, ready to knock over the world and everyone in it if necessary to justify his belief in me, I'd shouted, "Yes, Uncle Albert! Yes!" Only when around him did those intense feelings surface. Strange and unfamiliar, they splattered vivid colours in the air all around me.

Aware right now of a deepening silence, finding myself still standing on the landing at home, I suppressed my sense of joy at my memories and resumed my usual persona — flat, even aloof. Following Mom down the stairs and into the kitchen, I saw she had put breakfast things on the dining table and already had flour, sugar, butter, and all the ingredients necessary for baking a cake on the counter. Seeing me, she exhaled a huge sigh that puffed out her cheeks. I thought they looked exactly like the colour of the pastry she was kneading, and a new feeling of dread rose in me.

"Julian boy …"

"I'm not a boy! Whose birthday is it now?"

"Maybe I'm baking a cake for you." She said this with a smile in her voice. "Look at me. Why don't you ever talk to me or listen to me?" Now sorrow filled her voice, and I was amazed at the swiftness of the change. "I pray for you, you know, pray you'll find a fine profession and rise to the top in it. You do know, don't you, that I want you to be successful for your own sake?" With sudden hope flaring in her eyes, she asked, "What about the Royal Conservatory, since you've got a thing for pianos? You could take real lessons, not just what you get at school or from Uncle Albert. If you really worked at it, maybe you could get good enough to play on the stage."

And so she dreamed, hoped, maybe prayed some more. But praying hadn't saved any of her dead children. Later, as I passed the open door of my stillborn brother Jeremy's hallway room, I could smell aromas of lavender drifting from it. I held my nose to block it and groaned.

CHAPTER FIVE

I got back into bed that Saturday morning after delivering newspapers from Bayview Avenue to Yonge Street. As I huddled beneath my deep blue comforter, still cold from the biting wind outdoors, I thought about our house, how it was filled with empty bedrooms echoing with faint children's voices, with the flutter, the whispers, of pale curtains around the windows, of empty beds where the ghosts of stillborn babies lay, fledgling birds with the life stamped out of them and scarcely a chance to breathe even once.

Each baby's name hung above the door of the room, and the room itself was decorated with the child's imagined personality: Susannah's, pink and flowery, candles on the window ledge; Genevieve, who shared the room, had pink and yellow T-shirts framed and hung above her bed; Jeremy's room at the end of the hallway was blue, of course, with a miniature football sitting atop a white dresser. The creepiest thing was a plaster cast of a baby's white nightgown hung on a coat hanger attached to a wall hook. I assumed it was the one Genevieve had worn before dying. To me, our house and the people in it added up to absences. To the few people who knew about it, it was a ghost house, disturbing, upsetting, the whisperings from within and about it blending with the ghostly voices of dead children.

Uncle Albert's voice boomed down a tunnel of time: "For God's sake, Muriel! What the devil! Do you talk to them, too?

I suppose you sing to them and leave this poor kid to talk to himself or cry himself to sleep." He pointed out the door where I, feeling restless, kicked a ball about in the backyard, but could hear everything. Unfortunately, there was little he could do.

I loved Uncle Albert. When he spoke, I saw the prettiest colours of the rainbow, also soft purple shadows, sometimes spangled gold. But when he said those words to Mom, they hovered in the air, smeared over with black.

As I said, there was little he could do. My dad didn't try to change anything; he merely went along with it all and called the doctor for Mom only when he felt things were getting out of hand. When they did, his shoulder drooped. Sometimes his eyes were blank. His movements about the house were slow, jerky, as if he had to remember to move one foot in front of the other.

During my teenage years, I walked the seven blocks to Northern Secondary on Mount Pleasant Road. Dad had tried to get me to enroll in North Toronto Collegiate because he said it had a better academic record, but I persuaded him I was better off at Northern, since I'd gotten into the gifted program there in science and math. The real reason was that my friends, Jack and Robbie, were going there. Steve, too.

My ambling took me first past Dominion Coal and Wood on the corner, with its nine indomitable black-and-grey silos guarding the world around them in a kind of remote elegance, then by tennis courts on Davisville Avenue, movie theatres on Mount Pleasant Road, and many little shops of flowers and books as well as dry cleaning and pet stores that lined the busy road that ran in a straight line all the way north to Lawrence Avenue. Mount Pleasant Baptist Church stood white and imperturbable on the east side, the place where Mom had wandered in one of her crazy episodes. I wondered what kind of people went there.

One cool October afternoon I dawdled down Mount Pleasant Road, wanting to minimize the time before dinner when Mom would hang around me and peer over my shoulder while I did my homework. I stared into each shop window, idly speculating about the people who owned them — brave entrepreneurial types, I thought, or people with dreams. I watched as older people entered the Mount Pleasant and Regent movie theatres for 4:30 p.m. shows, while others negotiated the few steps into the church's open door. Passing the Davisville tennis courts, I heard not just the soft plop of tennis balls but also the pull of muscles and tendons. When roaming among people on the sidewalks, I caught the significance of a certain type of cough or sneeze, the creaking of old men's joints.

This was my life, I thought, until it wasn't, until a bully, followed by a beautiful snake, penetrated my admittedly disturbed universe.

That particular afternoon, again to delay going home, I continued south and through the cemetery gates. Rambling among headstones, monuments, and a cenotaph or two, I gorged myself with the sounds of the natural world: the voices of trees, the distress of newly mown grass, of blackbirds, swallows, cicadas. I also listened for the voices of the dead because I found a soothing quality in them, regardless of any violence or misery that might have caused their deaths. Some I could deduce as having had an ugly or sudden demise from words inscribed or from the birth and death dates indicating the sudden decease of a young person. In spite of it, peace settled over me as I threaded through them, a kind of tranquility that comes with acceptance of the moment, of whatever will be.

Suddenly, I heard a rude laugh, a snort, more laughter, then voices. "Oh, man, this is great stuff. You got any more? Where do'ya get it?"

"You buy it from me, man. You won't get a deal like this from nowhere."

The owners of the voices were behind a stone mausoleum a short distance from me, but I recognized Leon's, the foul-mouthed kingpin bully in our class. There always seemed to be one. He was in the cemetery dealing drugs to other boys! I feared Leon. I knew he hated me and wondered if it was because he sensed the contempt I held for kids like him: arrogant and stupid, yes, but also cunning. He often called me a nerd and sometimes tried to initiate fights with me. In his eyes, I was a loser, and in spite of my height, someone easy to pick on.

Right now, as I stiffened and held my breath, I heard a stifled exclamation followed by the noise of running feet. A few moments passed before Leon came from behind the stone slab and headed toward me, two younger boys trailing him. I could run, but Leon would further despise me. He would easily catch up with me, anyway, since I wasn't known for being fast on my feet. Damn everything to hell!

"Well, look at who we've got here! Mr. Big Creep himself." Leon's face opened into a delighted smile that was also a sneer. His eyes — strange how suddenly they reminded me of Steve's — two cold hard little pebbles set close together. His hair fell over his eyes, and he flicked it back with thick fingers. "Hanging around with the ghosts in here? Hey, you guys, you think he talks to them, too?" To me he said, "You want to do drugs, little big boy? Nah. The stuff we got ain't for weirdos." He thrust back his shoulders and flexed his arms, his sneer turning quickly to belligerence.

As I frantically weighed my options, I caught sight of a figure who reminded me of Steve. It slipped from behind a tree to disappear into the shadows. How could it be him? I shrugged it off. Back to my options: I was bigger than Leon, but he had his sidekicks with him, and Ricky, the smaller one, had a reputation for mean-spirited savagery. Then it came to me: I would try nonchalance. Fixing a smile on my face, I forced myself to walk toward them.

"I'm about to meet some other guys here and we've got our own stuff." I hoped only I could hear the tremor in my voice as I continued toward them diagonally, attempting at the last minute to march right past them.

"Hey! You don't get to strut by me like that!" Leon's voice had risen to a full-throated roar while his eyes were now narrow slits. A thin smile sliced across his face. "What other guys? Ha!" He swivelled to his mates. "This wacko kid is talking to the ghosts in here." He lost his smile and advanced toward me, then broke into a jog. At that moment, if a grave had opened up and swallowed me, I would have been grateful. But Leon stopped in his tracks at the sound of a motorbike swerving through the cemetery gates. It cruised slowly along the road that wound among the headstones, not far from where we were standing.

I'd been saved by a stranger on a bike. "See yah!" I yelled, punching the air and sprinting north toward the wooden walls and my backyard. I'd built footholds in that wall so that I could climb over it back and forth. Now I leaped but missed the first foothold, my right foot falling back onto something hard. Pain shot up my leg, and I cursed under my breath as I searched for the object I'd landed on. There, beneath my feet, half covered in creeping ivy, was a greyish-white stone plaque in the shape of a heart. I knew most of the names of those buried in this part of the cemetery but had never seen this one. Forgetting Leon and his gang, I leaned closer, pushed the ivy aside, and tried to read the words engraved on it.

Genevieve, beloved daughter of Richard and Muriel Whitely. Born July 4, 1947. Died November 19, 1947.

Oh, dear God! Familiar hot needles of pain shot through my skull. A sense of unreality washed over me and everything around me. The wooden walls, the trees, the headstones all blurred, moved, and changed shape the way clouds shift about. Feeling even the boundaries of myself dissolving, I clasped my arms on my chest tightly. How to reconcile that Genevieve lay in a cot upstairs in our house while that same baby's body disintegrated beneath this stone? Those dead babies were talked to, read to, songs were sung to them and their birthdays celebrated, yet here was Genevieve buried just over the wall from our backyard.

Maybe it was me living in a different kind of reality. Maybe I was hallucinating, and further spasms of pain shot through my head. My heart thumped rapidly, painfully. Were Jeremy and Susannah also buried here?

As I bent to further search the ground, I heard a shout from Leon, heard the sounds of heavy footsteps coming closer. I'd believed he wouldn't chase me, wouldn't dare to breach the walls of our backyard. But, surely, he'd never get his clumsy bulk over it, even with the footholds. Despite my fright, the image of him attempting it brought a laugh to my throat. Next thing I knew I was over the fence, crouching in our backyard and trying to stifle my heavy breathing. After a few minutes, the curses from the other side faded, telling me Leon and his friends had given up the chase. I collapsed in a chair at the bottom of the garden. When my heart stopped thudding and my breathing calmed, when I regained some composure, I sat back and strained to hear the ordinary, everyday sounds: squirrels, birdsong; the rustle of trees, of grass. I was also preparing myself for tuning out Mom's voice.

When eventually I got up and strolled along the side of the house, I saw Dad climbing the front steps and watched him slip through the doorway. I followed him, then halted on the top step. *This is my house*, I thought. *This is my father coming home from work. My mom is in the kitchen preparing dinner. Our transistor radio is playing old pop songs of the 1950s.* With a sense of normalcy returning, I observed Dad put down his briefcase inside the door, then head for the radio to fiddle with the dial.

I followed him in, vague thoughts forming about how little I resembled him. In my sixteenth year, I towered above him and could almost pick up his slight figure. "You get your height from your mother," he'd once said. Right now I watched him pick up his briefcase again and lay it carefully on the living room coffee table. He hesitated, then slowly went into the kitchen. Coming right behind him, I heard him say hello to Mom, who had her back to him at the stove, saw him move closer to her, put a hand on her shoulder, and give her a peck on the cheek. A long-practised gesture of reassurance, I understood, an old habit. Mom didn't turn her face away, and I released a breath. Things would be okay this evening.

But not for me that night. In my dreams, in my nightmare, I was a ghostly figure wandering in the cemetery among blackened tree trunks, through branches grabbing at me. I stumbled, fell to my belly, and began crawling, scrabbling the ground with my hands. My face was in the grass, in rough ground cover and dried leaves. There, beneath my fingers, I felt a cold, ragged-edged stone. Scraping off the weeds, I read its inscription. It said only "Sus." Susannah? Now, suddenly, I was flat on my back, buried under mounds of dirt alongside my sister, Genevieve, and the one called "Sus." Only my face rose above it. Like a ghost hovering above my half-buried body, I gazed at myself and saw inscribed on my forehead the words: "Julian Whitely, born March 7, 1954."

Terrified, my heart seemingly leaping out of my chest, I looked for the date of my death but couldn't find it. Frantically, in the gloom of that place, I peered again at my own face, at my forehead. It shone like a pale quarter moon.

But I discovered nothing else. Was I dead or alive? I woke up screaming, my heart thumping so furiously that I was sure it would explode. Not just my heart but my body felt as if it were splintering, and I bent over to grope for my legs, my feet. Then I hugged my arms tightly across my chest.

Mom, in her nightclothes, was beside my bed, pushing me back against the pillows. "What's wrong? Are you sick?" Her hair was tied in curlers, face pale and blotchy in the dim hallway light.

"Just a dream, actually a bit of a nightmare," I answered, my voice squeaking. But at her worried frown, I already felt better. She cared. She would look after me.

CHAPTER SIX

In my second year of high school, I spent late afternoons and evenings in the library typing other kids' essays for pocket money, or in the music room trying out the old Steinway piano, to me the most beautiful instrument in the world. Often I stood for ages admiring its ivory fingers all lined up, fifty-two white, thirty-six black, poised to create the most heavenly sounds with the touch of someone's fingers.

With Uncle Albert's belief in me like a song in my heart, slowly, painfully, with help from the school's music teacher, I practised major and minor scales, taught myself to read sheet music, and played some of it haltingly. I fooled around with sounds and harmonies and could even manage a few chords by ear. Now, fascinated with how sounds were produced, longing to understand exactly how the whole mechanism worked, I tinkered with the piano long after the school had emptied. The conversation in the kitchen with Mom and Uncle Albert came back to me, and what Uncle Albert had asked me: "Are you up to it?" He had meant all the work required to be a musician.

"Yes siree!" I'd said. Then I'd added, "But we don't have a piano for me to practise on."

"Everything in good time," he'd said.

I didn't see him after that for a couple of months but heard Mom tell Dad he'd gone to see my Uncle Robert, who had set up another print shop in Niagara Falls.

"Uncle Robert?" I asked, coming up from the basement where I'd been polishing a violin case, one Uncle Albert had been working on. Mom put down the phone receiver, and the two of us sat at the table across from each other, waiting for Dad. A slow cooker sat on the table, aromas of Mom's special blend of herbs that she grew in the garden rising from it. Mom's head nodded in time to Elvis Presley's "All Shook Up" — the words were a good description of her.

I took another quick glance to assess my chances of gleaning information about Uncle Robert, and Steve, for that matter. Often I'd been curious about this reclusive uncle, about his comings and goings and the silences that descended when it was known I was hanging about within earshot. I had never found the right time to ask. Now seemed a good time, but suddenly I wasn't sure I wanted to know how crazy our family really might be. Was there anyone in it who was not ... odd? Then, suddenly, just like that, I decided to go for it.

"Why does Uncle Robert never come here anymore?" I asked. "Did I hear you tell Dad he'd moved to Niagara Falls? Why do we never see him and Aunt Lindy? What about Steve? He's about the same age as me and nobody ever mentions him, like he doesn't exist."

Mom appeared confused for a moment. Her head stopped nodding, and when she looked at me, her eyes were flat. "I'll tell you another time."

"Why not now? How come they don't come here anymore?" I was on a roll. "I'm an only child. I've got one cousin, and everyone pretends he doesn't exist. Is there something the matter with him? What's going on, Mom? Whatever it is, I'm an adult. You *can* talk to me, you know."

Mom lowered her head in her hands, then suddenly jerked up. The flat look in her eyes changed to a gleam as the late-afternoon sun slanted through the venetian blinds.

"Don't you see Steve at school? Even though he doesn't go there anymore, I hear he gets together with his friends still."

"I was talking about Uncle Robert and Aunt Lindy. *They* never come here anymore."

Steve might still hang out with his old cronies at school, but I rarely saw him. He was a moving shadow, a square hulk disappearing around the corners of the building, always surrounded by a group of boys I had no desire to know. I looked across at Mom and was startled by the sudden rearrangement of her face. She seemed younger, even pretty.

"Julian?"

"Yes?"

"It works both ways, you know. Why don't *you* talk to me? You never tell me anything. I don't even know if you have any friends. So, do you?" Her eyes focused sharply on me, still with a glint in them.

"What kind of a question is that? Of course, I do."

"Well, then, why don't you bring them home and introduce them to me? Has it never occurred to you that I might like to meet them, the boys, or any girls, you hang around with? So, who are your friends? Where do they live? Do you have a girlfriend?"

Oh, dear God! She'd never asked me these questions before, and the changes in her were dizzying. Usually, I fell in with whatever frame of mind she was in, but at the moment I wasn't in the mood. About Uncle Robert, I'd have to ask Dad, and right now, find reasons to satisfy Mom why I never brought my buddies home.

"Jack's one of my friends," I began, sitting with my elbows on the table, trying to look anywhere but at Mom. "He lives up on Roehampton. We play chess, and you know, just fool around. When I finish building my raft, he's going to help me float it at Cherry Beach."

"The skinny one with red hair?" she asked. "I've seen

someone like that on the tennis courts." Her face was still bright with interest. "Okay. Who else?"

"There's Robbie. He and Jack play tennis, so you might have seen them together. We ... um ... the three of us hang around."

"What does that mean — hang around?"

"Uh, um, I don't know, we do guy stuff." I wished she would quit, because her questions seemed like an unhealthy kind of prying, but I did like that for once she was showing positive interest. Also, for once, her mood was mellow. Then Dad came in, gave her a peck on the cheek, nodded, and smiled at me.

Mom got up, lifted the lid from a casserole, and started serving it on our plates. A dish of steaming rice followed. "Okay, eat up your dinner." At the smile in her voice, the room lit up, golden beams falling all around us.

I took mouthfuls of rice and stew, almost choking over all the changes in Mom's moods. She remained bright and interested throughout dinner so, of course, Dad acted relieved and happy. And while I appreciated Mom's rare mood, and in some ways would like to have prolonged it, I couldn't think of any way to explain why I never brought my friends here. Suddenly, I only wanted to get up and go to my room. But then I'd have to pass my phantom sisters' room, so I slumped in my chair.

Eventually, Dad cleared the table, while Mom and I remained sitting at either end. Then, because of the conversation we'd been having earlier, plus her good mood, even because of my nightmare, I thought I might bring up the subject of the dead babies. It was ridiculous, totally absurd, that we never talked about it. I hesitated, and in the end, lacked the courage. Instead, because Mom had been expressing interest in my friends and what we did, I told her we often got together at Jack's house. We fooled around with his Yamaha piano, Jack on a set of drums.

A flicker of surprise, another flaring of hope I'd seen before, lit her greyish-green eyes. Maybe she was recalling what Uncle Albert had said about me, and knowing Mom, her mind would race on ahead. She'd cling to the hope that in time I might even become a concert pianist.

"How well can you play already?" The same glow sparked in her eyes.

I didn't know how to answer that. In fact, it felt strange to have such a normal conversation at all. I longed to tell her — to tell someone — that for me each key held a colour. When I heard E flat, it was dusky pink. F major was swathed in shades of green, and D minor was tinged with blue-grey. Tiny hammers striking the strings inside a piano produced sounds that caused me rare, intense emotion that sometimes teased, calmed, and consoled my heart. There was no way I could explain any of this to Mom, or Dad, because it would sound ridiculous. Only Uncle Albert understood. If I told Mom, she would pester me about it and drive me crazy. No doubt she'd think *I* was crazy, and obviously madness ran in this family.

All I said instead was: "I can play some stuff. Am I any good? Uncle Albert says I've got some natural talent but will need years and years of practising many hours every day to be any good."

Conflicting feelings crossed Mom's face, a shuddering at the idea that she would have to put up with all the practising. But she could also dream that by doing so I might become a famous pianist.

"Some people play by ear and get really good," she said, hope still reflected in her face.

"Yeah," I said, "but not even one percent of really good pianists ever get noticed or make it onto a concert stage."

Then one day, sometime after that conversation, Dad walked in from work and said, totally out of the blue, "Maybe we should get Julian a second-hand piano. He can fix it and practise on it."

CHAPTER SEVEN

"This is a very severe case of mumps." The family doctor's voice was gravelly, as though from a recent cold. "He's sixteen? Unusual at his age. Very severe case. I haven't seen one like it in years." When he said he feared I might get complications, that I could even end up sterile, Mom sank into the chair by my bed, an expression of white-faced defeat on her face. From beneath a starched white sheet, I heard her mutter about being a cursed woman. "Although this is rare," the doctor added hastily.

From that day on, Mom became fixed in her belief that I would never have children, so could never give her grandchildren. I absorbed it as my own truth and never questioned it. Eventually, Mom recovered from her near hysteria and a period of depression that followed, but our relationship altered. When she looked at me, hope and despair fluctuated in her expression, and I knew she was on a new mission to make something of me. Soon after that, she urged me to get a new haircut, buy new clothes.

"The hippie age is over," she told me. "Get some fitted shirts, a blazer." Then she popped up with various wild schemes. "If you like pianos so much, I'll even pay for you to take lessons." Another time she said, "Jules, in time you could even become well known, maybe even famous." Again into her eyes came that glint of hope. It warred with her disbelief, and I wanted to both laugh and cry.

∞

One day, toward the end of Grade 10, I was lounging near the school's main entrance, my eyes half closed. As I always did, I imagined all the feet that had walked along the stone path and through the huge oak doors to the building. I loved its Gothic entrance, all the sculpted grotesques attached to the inside and outside of the foyer. It was imposing, inspiring.

"You're the eternal observer," Jack teased me, not for what I saw but what I heard, the sounds of hundreds, even thousands, of people jostling in crowds, in lines, the noise of bodies of all shapes and sizes running, walking, dragging their feet. This particular day I heard a laugh that had a pitch, a colour and shape to it, that I'd not heard before. I followed the owner of it into the main hall.

It belonged to a girl called Louisa Blackstock, who had just transferred from a school in Oakville. To my delight, I discovered she was in my Grade 10 homeroom.

Louisa — soon a ripple shot through any place she inhabited: hallways, library, the playing fields behind the school and the pavement in front of it, even out to Mount Pleasant Road. Like most of the guys, I hung around to listen for her voice, for the laugh that floated on the air wherever she was. My mental images of her were the flip of an abbreviated dress, a bounce when she walked, a short, wide nose in a face that was never still, the swinging of fair hair that she liked to flick over one shoulder, sometimes to tie in a ponytail. A doll's face and figure, I thought. And her eyes: a shadowy green, the shade you might see under a weeping willow tree.

I was intrigued and heard the colours of her voice, her laugh — buttercup yellow, shimmering orange and magenta. I liked watching her whole-body animation, the energy, the joy and optimism that hung in the air wherever she was.

"What are you doing? Don't you ever go home?" Robbie

saw me sitting on one of the granite stones near the main entrance as he came out. I felt foolish and shrugged. "Well, don't you?"

At that moment Louisa's girlish laugh drifted toward us, and we both looked to the street where a knot of students surrounded her.

"Ah," Robbie said. "I get it." He paused. "What's stopping you joining them? I can see you breaking your heart to get near her."

I never could join such a group, of course, but I never tired of lingering on the periphery of those who always encircled her. I knew right away she wasn't for me, so sometimes I made an effort to block images, to tune out the sounds of her. That summer, after school finished, it was easier. Louisa went up north to a girls' camp while I remained in the city working with Uncle Albert tuning pianos, and repairing instruments in our basement as a hobby. I also continued my work on the wooden raft, and when Uncle Albert came over, I helped him chip away at the frame of a harpsichord, plus a small violin. He also repaired various kinds of wind instruments. I knew Mom didn't like the noise we often made, but we couldn't work on these things at Uncle Albert's place because the neighbours would hear everything through the apartment's walls.

"Well, Jules, some of my genes must have slipped sideways and landed on you," Uncle Albert said to me one afternoon. "We have similar tastes, but you've definitely got a better ear." He slapped me on the shoulder, his eyes teasing, full of warmth. Other times he'd say, "Come on, Julian, stand up straight. You're a tall, good-looking fellow and you'll yet have the world at your feet — whatever your mother thinks." His eyes twinkled. "Never mind her. She's a good woman." Under his breath he added, "Or means to be."

I hero-worshipped Uncle Albert. Unlike the usual image

of a musician, even one who went to people's homes to fix their instruments, he dressed in a tweed jacket over smart dark jeans — a businessman and an artist mixed together, a man not willing to be labelled.

"You're so like him!" Mom yelled one day as Uncle Albert and I came upstairs for coffee, exasperated by the frequent twanging of violins that floated upstairs from the basement, by the squawking of the flutes and trumpets we were fixing.

"Mom, you know Uncle Albert can't take instruments home," I said in defence of both of us. "His neighbours will complain ..."

"So the neighbours count, but not me? Look at the pair of you — big ears always listening for something, God only knows what. Can't a woman get a bit of peace even in her own house?"

Uncle Albert gave her a placating smile and told her she looked wonderful, even though at that moment she had curlers in her hair. "Okay, Julian," he said, "enough with polluting the air. Let's move on to woodwork." And the two of us returned to the basement, he to work on his half-finished woodcarvings, me on my raft.

That wasn't all I did that summer. Jack and I saw a few movies. Robbie came over and we played cards, sometimes chess. Jack and I drove up and down Yonge Street on Friday nights, the two of us balanced on his old motorbike, Jack roaring above the noise of his bike, traffic, and people, "Groovy, man! Groovy!"

And so the summer slipped by, with Louisa becoming a misty shadow hovering only peripherally in the margins of my mind.

∞

Around dinnertime, just before the new school year began, a truck pulled into our driveway. I was sitting on the top step, not yet willing to go inside and face a barrage of the usual questions from Mom: "How was your day? Made any new friends?"

Three stocky men climbed out and began to unload a piano. Mom came to the door in her gardening clothes, hair wrapped in a scarf. Embarrassed at being seen like that, horrified when she learned a piano was being delivered to our address, she yelled, "Take the thing away! There's already enough cacophony going on in our house."

Uncle Albert pulled up in his car behind the truck and jumped out. He winked at me, but when he spoke to Mom, he struck a firm note. "Now look here, Muriel. You want Julian to make something of himself, don't you? *Don't* you?" He stood directly in front of her, brow furrowed. "Your only son enjoys music, pianos — all the musical instruments, in fact — and he's got talent, potentially a lot. For God's sake, give him a chance to succeed in something he loves."

The piano went into the basement, and in a frenzy I ripped off its wrapping — and stared. It was an old wooden model, made of hard maple I guessed, but with what looked like pure ivory keys, yellowed and a bit chipped. My joy overwhelmed me so that for the longest time I simply stood gazing at it.

"Built around the 1930s, I'd say." Uncle Albert had been dealing with the mover and now came running down the stairs. "Look at these beauties." Reverently, he ran his fingers over the keys, striking a resounding C major chord. "These will spoil you for playing on any of the new ones that are made mostly of acrylic plastic. What say I teach you how to tune it and you can practise to your heart's content?"

Over time, Uncle Albert and I pulled the piano apart and put it together again. I learned the piano's history, how it was first developed in 1700, and became the culmination of all other stringed instruments.

"It's the most complicated of any instrument and has the broadest range," Uncle Albert said. "I bet you didn't know that all music composed for other instruments can also be played on a piano."

"I love it!" I said, suddenly realizing I was becoming more comfortable with my feelings of joy. This piano was the greatest gift in the world, the greatest on all the planets in the solar system, and excitement rose in me when I thought how I could explain its working to Dad.

"A piano is a keyboard stringed instrument," I told him that night. The two of us stood with the lid to the piano open. I had the back open, too, and pressed a few keys to show how each one was struck by a hammer. "But the tricky thing is that the hammer mustn't remain in contact with the string or it will dampen the sound. See how each one moves away from the string at once, then returns to its original position, but not violently, so it can be played again immediately after it's depressed …?"

"So the same note can be played again and again very fast," my dad finished for me, running his fingers over the keys, up and down, up and down, until Mom yelled down the basement steps for us to quit the damn noise.

CHAPTER EIGHT

Two weeks of Grade 11 passed before Louisa returned to school. I dubbed the way she skipped into my English literature class "The Advent of Louisa" due to the commotion that accompanied her, her laugh, the noise of other students jockeying to be near her, all of them talking and laughing at once.

Hyenas, I thought sourly.

In hot pants and skimpy tank tops despite the early autumn coolness, Louisa bounced into my history class one morning. She wriggled her hips, shook her hair that fell in ringlets over her eyes, and jiggled into a seat to put her hands behind her head and stare at everyone and no one.

My eyes scarcely left her when we were in the same classes. Outside, I followed the sound of her voice that came to me in shades of dazzling white and gold. I saw her everywhere, around corners and at the edges of things, but when I searched for her, she was nowhere.

Fall deepened into winter and she exchanged her hot pants, sometimes for bell-bottomed jeans, other times for black leggings and boots that reached her thighs. Tight-fitting woollen sweaters outlined her breasts. One day I was surprised to see she had cut her hair very short, that she had painted her face. In classrooms, in hallways, and outdoors, her singsong voice floated. She had witty words for everyone. The only places I never saw her were on the sports fields or tennis and basketball courts. Somehow I couldn't imagine her getting rough and dirty, physically tangling with other kids over a basketball.

Fellows from different grades with muscular shoulders, shiny foreheads, and pimply faces continued to elbow one another to get near her and carry her books. The lucky ones escorted her on a date. Leon, the school's star football player, and to me, a classic bully type, became the most successful, probably because he was the most forceful. Lately, he'd taken to wearing light blue jeans with the words I GOTTA BE ME written all over them in red. I noticed how a hard, metallic look entered his eyes whenever he approached her, how he shoved others aside to get to her. He followed her everywhere, his hands always touching her. It disgusted me to see it, and I wondered why she didn't tell him to get lost. Whenever she did walk away, arm in arm with another boy, Leon glared after them, his sandy hair greased up from his forehead, hands in his pockets, that flinty look in his eyes. Always watching from the fringe, I saw how he balled his fists when she skipped off with his friend, Ronnie, wriggling her hips and pulling at her short hair as she went, her fluting voice echoing after her.

Long afterward I thought of her as one of those girls who become the stuff of legend, popular among both sexes — and teachers, too. Some called her "Twiggy" for the slightness of her build. Others said "Hairpin," "Toothpick," or "Flirt." She didn't care. I hung around long after she'd gone as though still absorbing her presence, my blood pounding in my veins. But I felt no jealousy when she favoured another guy, because she wouldn't even know I existed. If she did, she'd never go for me. I admitted to myself, though, that there were uncomfortable moments when I wasn't sure I even liked her due to the way she behaved.

One cold, breezy day in front of the school, I spotted Louisa surrounded by a clutch of male Grade 12 and Grade

13 students, her eyes roving over all of them. She looked bored. Tapping her boot on the pavement, she constantly turned her head to glance around her. Abruptly, she spun on one heel, caught my eye, and flashed me a quick smile that kept me awake that night, and many more later. After that I didn't care for anything, only to steal a glimpse of her, to hear her laugh, to see the sun light up her doll-like face. It was enough for me to know she existed somewhere in the universe to admire and dream about.

The months slid toward spring, a late and very frosty one. Not much changed until one particular day. It happened on the sidewalk outside Ted's Soda at the corner of Mount Pleasant and Eglinton. Only two months remained to the end of school, to holidays, and for me, to summer school to study university-level math. After that, to work with Uncle Albert.

A late light snow had fallen, and the air was frigid. Despite that, and as always, a knot of older students gathered at that busy intersection and now crowded in and outside Ted's. All were animated, loud, laughing, some swearing. Leaning up against the restaurant's north wall, I daydreamed. A wan sun broke through the clouds to warm my uplifted face, and I tuned in to the sounds of birds, of boots tramping the snow, of bits of ice falling off tree branches, until I heard a familiar voice giving a high-pitched shout: "No! I said no! Not ever — never!"

Through an accumulating crowd, I sensed the spectator's hunger for a scene and edged closer. When the girl's voice rose to a shout, when a male voice let loose a string of vulgar language, without thinking, I flung myself into the centre of a knot of students. Louisa stood flushed and angry, fists balled like a boxer's against Leon. Fright was written all over her. The kingpin's hair had fallen over his forehead, so I couldn't see his eyes, but his nostrils flared and his mouth twisted into an ugly snarl. Louisa's thin arms flailed against him. Leon grabbed them, two flying white limbs that looked as if they'd snap at a touch. He spat words about her promising to go with him. I searched the crowd for any sight of teachers, any adult who might intervene.

The number of students watching increased, but no one did anything — dumb spectators hoping for excitement. Leon ripped off Louisa's blue woollen hat, grabbed her hair, and pulled her against him, pinning her arms.

Something sharp lodged in my brain. Without thought or plan, I found myself in the centre of a group, swinging at Leon. Next thing my fists were on his chest, in his face, and suddenly he was on the curb, the school bully lying at my feet, bleeding into the snow. A collective gasp flew into the air, astonishment, dismay — I wasn't sure who or what it was directed at. Some in the crowd regarded me strangely before they moved away. I was a solitary figure, a lone sentry guarding a body on the pavement, since even Leon's mates had left. At first elation filled me. Although I didn't recognize the person who had just accomplished this feat, I thought that if I got to know him, I'd like him.

CHAPTER NINE

My transformation afterward went instantly from gawky guy-on-the-sidelines to hero. I had slain the brash bully, though in truth we were about the same size. For a few days, nudges and whispers floated after me. Louisa's greenish eyes were on me, full of curiosity and sudden respect, but Leon's hatred burned like black ice in eyes that were still bluish-black and puffy where I'd hit him. I could all but hear revenge rattling in his bones and knew it would only be a matter of time before he came after me.

"Julian, thank you," Louisa said. "Yesterday I think maybe you saved my life." Her elfin form was beside me outside the main school doors, small face tilted upward. That voice fell across my ears as a sweet caress. As she touched my arm, I tried to say something, but nothing came out of my mouth.

Shuffling my feet, not knowing what to do with my arms, I crossed them, then immediately figured that was rude. I thrust my hands in my pockets, but thought that wouldn't do, either, so let them dangle at my sides. Mute, embarrassed, completely ignorant of what was expected of me, I was about to turn away from her when again she tapped my shoulder.

"Hey, big boy, aren't you even going to talk to me?" Her eyes, which had turned the colour of molasses in the late-afternoon sun, were filled with curiosity. She swung her arms as she studied me.

"Of … of course, I'd be happy to talk to you anytime."

I'd mumbled this without looking at her, loathing myself for how I probably appeared. Then a comforting notion hit me, that maybe she'd appreciate a guy who didn't jump all over her. But depressing thoughts followed: *She'll just want to prove she can conquer me the way she has with all the other boys. Soon enough she'll forget big hero me.* I couldn't think what to say, so I shrugged, did my best to smile at her — a stupid sickly one — and said I had to go. As I began to walk off, I sneaked a quick glance over my shoulder. Louisa, with slow footsteps, her shoulders drooping, was moving away. Elation filled me as I straightened my own.

While I remained indecisively on the corner of Broadway and Mount Pleasant, an odd feeling came over me, as if someone's eyes were boring into me, and I spun around. Louisa's older sister, Pam Blackstock, stood a few feet from me. She was a tall, willowy girl with jet-black hair and ice-blue eyes in a pale face — not anything like Louisa. If I'd thought of her at all, it had been as a young shepherdess wandering over faraway green hills, a crook in one hand, books in the other. Right now we held each other's gaze.

"If you want my advice," she said coolly, "you shouldn't mess with my sister." She shrugged eloquently as her eyes held mine a moment longer before she turned and walked off.

I had no clue what she was talking about, didn't want to know, and immediately forgot her.

After that, Louisa began to seek me out, but I couldn't think how to respond. Then came the day after a biology class when I walked through the school halls toward the main doors and she darted out of her classroom, breezing up to me. Taking both my hands, she asked, "Hey, Jules, are you avoiding me or something?"

I flushed, then mumbled, "No, of course not. Did you run out of class — just like that?"

She laughed. "Who cares? Want to go on a date somewhere?"

A date? I could scarcely look at her.

"I ... well, I d-don't know much about dating," I stuttered, "but ... maybe I could hang out with you, like, right now? If that's okay?" Next thing we were sitting side by side on a park bench on Broadway Avenue near Mount Pleasant, shoulders almost touching. I was in agony, wondering what to talk about, what people did when they said they "hung out" — if that was what we were doing. Louisa's face was close to mine. Sweat formed on my cheeks and upper lip, and embarrassed, I looked away from her. To my surprise, she placed her hands on my red-hot cheeks and turned me to face her. Smiling into my eyes, she touched my hair, ran her fingers over my eyebrows, picked up one of my hands, then dropping it, flicked her hair over her shoulder in the seductive gesture I'd seen many times before.

Desperate to say something, I blurted, "Look, Louisa, I really don't know what you want with me. I ... I don't know anything about you, like, what your hobbies are or the things you most like to do. Maybe we could talk about school and the courses we like the most. Don't I — we — need to know some of these things about each other so we can have a conversation, you know, to *hang out*?"

Louisa released a long breath, and the usual teasing light in her eyes faded and was replaced with surprise. "No one ever asks me stuff like that."

I waited for more, but she remained silent, and I wondered if I'd asked too many questions in my eagerness to know too much too soon. "You don't have to say anything if you don't want to," I said, then hit upon what should be a safe subject. "What about your classes? What's your favourite subject?"

"Oh, who cares about school!" A look of scorn sparked in her eyes. "Hobbies? I suppose I must have one. Everyone seems to. Why do you want to know? Do *you* have any?"

"Yes, lots. I like music, the piano. I sculpt things out of

wood and have started on cases for musical instruments. Right now I'm working on building a raft — a big one."

"Oh," she said, her voice flat.

I waited for more. Discomfort that I'd offered all this and gotten nothing in return settled on me. Louisa gazed into the distance and restlessly swung her legs. In the stretching shadows, the two of us sat silhouetted, both together and apart. An uncomfortable silence spread between us.

Moments passed, then Louisa, dropping her usual lilting, little-girl voice, faced me. With her hands flying in the air for emphasis, she launched into a monologue about fashion, hairstyles, and makeup. "I want to be a designer of clothes," she said with importance. "Or a cosmetician. You know why? Because the look of a person — how they dress, how they do their makeup — tells you almost everything about them, don't you think?"

I took stock of her. She wore a short tight skirt of denim material with a sloppy sweater over it. Red leggings reached down to shiny black slip-on shoes. She levelled her heavily pencilled eyes at me, and I started. In a sliver of pale sunlight from parting clouds, her eyes had become the colour of a stagnant pond. Her sister's words came back to me, telling me I shouldn't "mess" with Louisa, and involuntarily I inched away on the park bench.

"So what are you telling me — telling the world — about yourself when you wear those clothes and put on that makeup?"

"You're not supposed to tell I'm wearing any," she said, but I knew she was pleased I'd noticed. "And really, Julian, tell me honestly, have you ever noticed what I wear? Seriously, have you?" Her eyes remained intently on mine.

"Not really, I guess, until now." Did boys generally notice what girls wore? Sitting on the park bench beside a girl who definitely knew how to dress, how to do makeup, I knew I was out of my depth.

"Hey, look at you!" Louisa laughed as she cupped my burning face in her hands. "But listen, why wouldn't you decorate the most important thing — yourself — in the most beautiful and different way you can think of?" Next thing she was off the table and strutting before me. She shimmied her body, tilted her head at various angles, and formed her lips into an O.

"Yes, I suppose so," I began, embarrassed at what she was doing, both hating and loving it at the same time.

"Don't look like that, you square! Can't you tell I'm imitating being a model on a catwalk? Oh, but I don't suppose you know what that is. You really are an innocent, aren't you?" She laughed again, not her usual high-pitched, tinkling voice but a throaty one. She dropped the seductive pose, and with a voice now filled with earnestness, said, "What I really want to do is decorative kind of stuff, you know, painting, make things beautiful."

"Well, your mother must be pleased that you know so early what you want to do. She must be proud of you."

"Ha! Like I would ever get noticed around our house." Louisa then launched into an account of her family, telling me she was the fourth sibling among seven. There were still no traces of the mannerisms or the affectations of voice and gesture so familiar to me.

"Seven kids," I breathed. "You're so lucky. I'd love to have a big family like that."

"No, you wouldn't! You'd hate all the messiness. I have to go and do something daring or stupid to get noticed, don't I? I get hand-me-down clothes, ugh, like every year ..." She pulled a face. My glance at her clothes suggested there was little hand-me-down about them.

"Oh, and if I do get a prize, like for some design work, nobody wants to know. Mom, in her usual distracted voice, says, 'Good girl, Lou.' I hate being called Lou!" She continued talking about missing clothes and school reports, sisterly fights resulting in many bruises, and once a broken tooth.

I had certainly pushed a hot button. Longing to keep her beside me, I changed the subject. "Tell me more about the kind of artwork you do. Like, do you also paint landscapes, people?"

"I already told you, didn't I?"

"No ..."

"Sometimes I paint landscapes. And you know, change things so they look better."

"And people? Do you draw or paint them?"

"No. You can't change them. People don't change."

You can't change people. People don't change. Words to remember. At the moment I was so entranced, so flattered she was honouring me with all these confidences, that I just wanted to sit there until the end of time and listen to her real voice, not the one she used for everyone else. It didn't really matter what she said.

But Louisa restlessly looked around her, which I interpreted as her having had enough of me and wanting to be gone. *On to the next guy*, I thought, with a return of the sour feeling I'd had before. I didn't know what else to say or do, and for a few moments more we remained seated on the park bench, both of us silent, Louisa swinging her legs and twisting her head. All around us students started dispersing, and the sounds of traffic dwindled.

Eventually, Louisa faced me again, cocked her head, and curved her painted lips into the half-smile that gave her what I called her come-hither look. The brief glimpse I'd seen of a Louisa unaffected, naked as it were, was gone. In a moment, physically she would disappear, too, but I had a few questions I urgently wanted to ask: Why did she tease and flirt with all the boys when she knew she didn't mean anything by it — or did she? A girl like her was called a siren, a seductress.

Did she know that, and if she did, did she care? I didn't ask, though. At that moment, continuing to feel swept up by the tide of her energy, like a helpless twig, I had other questions, dark thoughts, popping into my mind, such as: Was I merely a challenge to her, a guy to be conquered like all the others? Would our relationship, whatever it was, vanish any minute? Would a girl like her ever seriously look at me?

Conflicted, uncomfortable, not knowing what I should do next, I stood and told her I had to go home.

"Mommy's waiting?" She arched her brows. "Tomorrow then?"

Before I'd made a move to leave, Louisa had already floated away in the damp autumn air, her light jacket flapping behind her.

In the days and weeks that followed, Louisa's big eyes were always on me as she continued to seek me out. *It's because I don't fall all over her that she's interested in me*, I thought. But still her singsong voice fell softly on my ears, like the draw of a bow across a string. When near her, a miniature sun seemed to wrap itself around me. I took to listening for her "vibes," which probably sounded corny, but I believed people communicated in ways they weren't aware of. I tried to pick up their essences — their souls — but I couldn't decipher Louisa's.

CHAPTER TEN

That summer I grew up ... in a manner. Uncle Albert took me with him to tune pianos in Rosedale, Forest Hill, and Lawrence Park. Those swanky houses in upscale areas of the city struck me as filled with bored housewives, a parade of middle-aged blondes relieved only by an occasional brunette. All wore enough makeup to grease the wheels on a bicycle. They hung about us, pretending to be busy attending to some object in the room. Or just stood watching, fidgeting. Others flitted in and out, exclaiming about the weather, husbands, the kids. Uncle Albert ignored it all, finished tuning, bowed, smiled, and left.

On an overcast morning in late July, we drove to a forbidding-looking mansion on Lawrence Avenue East. Massive stone steps flanked by grey Doric columns led to an oak-panelled door. After Uncle Albert banged on the door, a woman I guessed to be in her mid-forties opened it and stood just inside. I stared as though at an apparition. She wore a see-through gown that could have been a nightdress. Leaning against the door frame as we passed through, she batted black eyelashes at me before giving a cursory nod to Uncle Albert. As her eyes continued to rove over me, heat rose in my face, and I glanced quickly at Uncle Albert.

He frowned and cleared his throat. "This is my nephew, Julian. He's as qualified as I am, perhaps more, but he needs —"

"Chaperoning." The woman's laugh was throaty, and

as she pirouetted, her gossamer-like gown spun above her knees.

"Let's see about the piano, shall we?" Uncle Albert's voice had become curt, and the smile had disappeared from his face.

The woman hovered as we worked. We found nothing wrong with her shiny Yamaha grand, and when we said so, she exclaimed, "Oh, but you must come regularly to check on it. The young fellow will do. Send him by himself next time." She nodded at me and winked.

Heat rose again in my face. I hunched my big shoulders and twisted my hands. Uncle Albert raised an eyebrow and gave the woman his usual little bow, but once outside and in his Ford station wagon, he chuckled. "A shame really how bored these housewives get. Their kids are at school, hubby is away in the downtown towers all day — and probably weekends someplace else."

I'd picked up all the vibes myself and thought that those beautiful mansions fairly groaned under the weight of unhappiness and boredom inside them.

"I'd send them all out to work," Uncle Albert added, "find something for them to do."

As summer faded, so did its harmonious notes, its beautiful lethargy. Discordant sounds with dirty colours attached to them snuck in at the edges of my thoughts. Lately, Mom had been behaving erratically. She often looked at me as though she disliked me. Other times she acted as if she wasn't sure who I was. Once, when I came in from a school music lesson, she glanced up from the romance novel in her lap and seemingly assessed me up and down the way you would a stranger. I couldn't begin to explain the conflicting emotions warring inside me, only that I felt like a gangling idiot being judged and a price put on me.

We gazed across the space between us, each considering

the other, then averted our eyes. A dull ache, beginning at the back of my throat, settled in my chest as the chasm of silence stretched between us. How hard it was to communicate with her!

But eventually Mom did break the silence. She tossed aside her novel, smoothed the folds of her dress, glared at me, and said, "You don't act like my boy." Her voice was accusing and high-pitched, not like hers at all. "You don't look like him. What are you doing in my house?"

Shocked, I swallowed air and almost choked, expecting anything but this. "Mom ... I'm Julian. Who do you think I am?"

"That's just it, I don't know." A bored look came over her face. "Do I want to know you? Why don't you just go away? My babies will be waking soon. I must get up and look after them, get their dinner ready."

I glanced up the staircase, and momentarily colluding in this fantasy, or whatever it might be called, I cocked my head to listen for the sounds of babies waking. My brain screamed. Familiar hot needles stabbed inside my skull, and I knew I couldn't stay in that house a moment longer. I ran outdoors and went to the Mount Pleasant Theatre where I watched *The Good, the Bad, and the Ugly*. Coming home late, I headed straight up to my room and lay awake, staring at the four walls. And there they were, tiny ghosts sliding along them. Baby sounds came from them, crying, gurgling, fussing noises, mixed with creepy adult weeping. Spooked, I put my head under my pillow but didn't sleep at all that night. The next morning, tired, my eyes inflamed, I remained under the covers, wary of going downstairs for fear of what I might find.

You're crazy! I wanted to yell at Mom. I couldn't imagine what had gotten into her head. Someone had to seriously speak to Dad about her. He should have done something long ago. But I felt sorry for him, too. For weeks now he'd been walking around looking depressed, and when I asked, "What's up, Dad?" hoping he'd tell me he'd done something about Mom, like talking to her doctor or was intending to, he just told me everything would be okay and not to worry.

My feelings were locked up tightly inside me. The only way to deal with them was to play with numbers in my head and conjure beautiful, clean equations.

The morning after that dreadful night, when eventually I came downstairs, Mom was making toast and coffee. She smiled at me and asked how I'd slept. Freaked, I thought there must be two people living inside her, and even she might not know at any moment which one was going to pop out.

After that, to avoid being home with her, I disappeared into the basement to practise scales on the piano or teach myself a new piece of music. In the afternoons, I hung out with Jack and Robbie. Some days we walked in the cemetery. Once, in the distance, I heard Leon's voice mingling with Steve's. *It can't be*, I thought. *Surely, Steve doesn't hang with him.* Other times my friends and I haunted Mount Pleasant Road. We saw movies at the Regent and Mount Pleasant movie theatres, played chess and card games, and on Friday nights, roared down Yonge Street. In those days, it was a young fellow's rite of passage. Jack and Robbie perched on Robbie's motorbike, while I drove my dad's car. They raced ahead of me, but I could easily pick out Jack with his flyaway red hair streaming from underneath his helmet. We made a strange trio: Robbie dark-haired with a squarish build, broad shoulders, and almost as tall as I was, but who slouched as though to minimize his height. Myself, tall, sort of fair, gangly, and wiry. Jack with his distinctive hair, thin arms, legs akimbo, reminding me of a marionette. Kids at school dubbed the three of us "The Nerds."

Mom's moods still swung from normal to weird, and I

never knew what I would find each time I returned home. I felt responsible for her until Dad got in from work; he'd told me to always come right home to check on her.

One late afternoon it was hot and humid, unusual for summer's end. Sweat trickled down my back and soaked my shirt as I glided south on my bike. I swiped my hand across my forehead to prevent moisture dripping into my eyes. I'd noticed during the day how clouds had shifted, how angrily they had changed shape and hue, from ugly purplish-black to blood-red. How could that be? I felt anxious and uneasy. The air was suffocating, but despite that, I picked up speed as I raced home.

Although I was supposed to check on Mom from time to time, today, as I got closer to our house, I just couldn't face whatever might be happening in it. *To hell with her!* I thought, and ditching my bike against the hedge along the side of our house, I returned to Mount Pleasant Road. Walking slowly, hot and agitated, I hoped to distract myself by enjoying the colours of birdsong and listening for the sound of trees groaning under the burden of mature leaves preparing to fall. For a while, I sat above the tennis courts, still delaying my return home.

When eventually I dragged my feet back along Merton Street, I spotted Dad on the top step of our house, a solitary, diminished figure, and despite the heat, his face pale. His head twisted as he glanced up and down and rocked back and forth on his heels. I rushed up the steps to him, thinking he was about to topple.

"Dad! What's wrong? Why are you … something's happened, hasn't it?" Maybe all the babies had died a second time, and with all my heart and soul, I fervently wished they had, that someone had come and torn them from the walls, tossed them out of their cots, had *killed them off*!

Shocked by my violent thoughts, I made an effort to

suppress my feelings. Dad was still swaying on his feet and didn't seem to see me, so I said again in a louder voice, "Dad!"

"Oh!" Startled, he stopped wobbling. "You, Julian. Your mom's missing." His voice had no emotion in it; in fact, he appeared spaced out, but all the time craned his neck up and down the street.

"Gone where?"

"I don't know, do I? I got home from work and couldn't find her anywhere in the house — not in the garden, not on the street." He stared blankly around him. "Have you seen her anywhere at all?" I avoided the dazed look in his eyes. Then his whole body snapped straight and he demanded, "Where were *you*?"

As though I were my mother's keeper! "I was at Robbie's house working on something. How long has Mom been ... gone?" And I answered myself with a mean thought: *She's been gone in the head most of her life.* But all I asked was: "Have you called the police?"

"I waited for a while," he said, his voice resuming that peculiar flatness. "I called your Uncle Albert, but I think he's still travelling in Quebec. As soon as it got dark, I did call the police. I think, I hope to God, they'll be here in a few minutes."

"What about the neighbours? Did you ask them?"

The look he shot me said: "You should know better. We don't tell the neighbours our business."

Within minutes of our brief exchange on the porch, two policemen arrived in a cruiser. Dad gave them a brief account of Mom and then said he and his son — he pointed at me — would search the cemetery because we were familiar with it and would know where to look.

One of the officers was young and raised an eyebrow, while the older cop shrugged. "If she's in there and you've got any idea where, go ahead," the younger one said.

Immediately, the two of us jumped over the back fence and into the cemetery's quiet gloom. Under a full moon that seemed to touch the tops of headstones, I thought I saw something white, and thinking it might be Mom in her old dressing gown, shouted, "Mom!"

"Don't shout," Dad said. "You might frighten her."

A fellow wearing a white shirt emerged from the darkness and gave us the finger as he walked past.

The police also searched the cemetery but didn't find her. I ran up and down our street and the neighbouring ones, while Dad lingered around the front porch, pale and helpless. I knew he felt he'd failed in the primary duty of his life: to protect his wife. Joining him, I stood with him and entertained a vision of us helplessly guarding an empty coffin.

The time was now about eleven. The sky beyond the street and city lights had darkened, and a cool wind knocked the branches of a maple tree against the roof of our house. Ominous clouds were forming, and the heat still scorched. Jumping up and down the steps, restless and agitated, I continued to peer into the gloom. Then, an hour later, maybe more, in the dim glow of the street lamps, a figure with an awkward gait limped along our street. My eyes popped as the figure came closer, something flapping around its legs. Holy Mother of Mary! A ghost had risen from its tomb beyond the back fence and was lurching up our street! The apparition approached nearer still. And then I saw it: the white of Mom's old dressing gown, the one with the tiny violets embroidered on it. On this warm evening, she was in her dressing gown! I remembered that the gown had been Dad's gift to her on the birth of Genevieve, and she had worn it all the years since. Mom had curlers in her hair and wore socks but no slippers.

Tapping Dad's shoulder, I pointed. "Mom." I said in a whisper, so I wouldn't frighten her.

"Muriel." Dad's voice was equally soft. He rushed down

the steps and tenderly took her arm. "You've been for a walk, dear, and now it's time for bed."

Mumbling to herself, Mom allowed us to lead her into the kitchen. Dad straightened, larger now, more authoritative again as he resumed the role of protector. He spoke gently, asking if she was cold and if she wanted something to drink. When she shook her head, he escorted her upstairs to bed.

After Dad dealt with Mom, he came back down to see the young police officer leaning against the closed front door of our house, half asleep. "Thank you very much, sir," Dad said. Startled, the officer opened his eyes and straightened. "My wife suffers from depression and I'll be sure to get her taken care of." Dad stood then, awkward and depleted once more. He shuffled his feet, not looking at me or the policeman until the officer was gone. Then, briefly, he raised his eyes to me, and without saying anything, headed for the stairs. "She's got some pills from before," he said over his shoulder. "Sedatives, I think. I'll give her one."

Later that evening he said, "I'll be getting the family doctor in tomorrow," and all that night he slumped in an armchair in front of a blank television, his face as vacant as the screen. Because we'd never spoken about Mom, there was now too much to say, nowhere to begin.

I slipped upstairs, hurried past the closed doors of the babies' rooms, shut my door, and locked it. Sleep eluded me. A gusting wind rattled the branches of the maple against the window, and above that noise, I thought I heard faint baby cries. Finally, I sat up, opened my eyes, and searched around me. There, dancing along the bedroom walls, were the silhouettes of dead babies gliding, their tiny nightdresses flapping, their crying mouths little black holes. I wanted to scream, to throw things at them. Instead, I pulled an old sweater over my head and scuttled downstairs to spend the remainder of the night at the kitchen table, head propped in my hands, waiting for dawn and sanity to return to our house.

CHAPTER ELEVEN

Dad came down to the kitchen at about seven the next morning. He looked terrible, as if he hadn't slept at all, either, his face still deathly pale, his eyes red.

"I'll stay home from work today to wait for the doctor," he told me in a monotone. "Your mom will stay in bed. You go off and do what you have to do." He made coffee and popped two slices of bread in the toaster, asking if I wanted any. Neither of us regarded the other directly.

By eight, Dad was on the phone to the family doctor. After he hung up, he stood in the middle of the kitchen, gazing into space.

"He wants her to go into hospital, doesn't he?" I asked.

Frozen in place, Dad continued to stare at nothing. He seemed not to hear me, nor even notice I was there.

"Dad?"

"Eh?" When he raised his eyes, they were sunk into their sockets and filled with pain. "I thought it would fade and eventually go away," he said under his breath. "I thought she would get better in time."

"Dad?" I said again.

We were father and son but had no ability to communicate, especially about something we'd never properly identified. Over the years, we'd pretended Mom's condition didn't exist. My feelings now were a complicated blend of fear and relief at the thought that if Mom had to go to a hospital, she'd be out of the house for a while at least. And maybe she'd get better. Perhaps even all the stuff about her dead babies might go away. *Oh, please, God, please!*

"Will Mom have to go to a hospital?" I repeated.

Finally, Dad glanced at me. "Julian, things aren't very good, I'm afraid. When I talked to the doctor just now, he said something about your mom having a psychotic depression. I don't know what that means exactly, but it sounds pretty serious. He said she doesn't need to be hospitalized for now, that he'll put her on medication and adjust it if he needs to. We'll just watch her to make sure she doesn't wander off again. In the meantime, we'll have to wait and see what the drugs do. I know school's starting again soon, but I don't want you to hang around after classes. Please come straight home, okay?"

Freaky, freaky, I get to hang around the house, around Mom, I thought. "I suppose so. Okay, I guess." I edged out the door. "Dad, why don't I ... I have to go and do something, I'll be back in a while." I had nothing in mind except to get out of the house.

When I eventually went upstairs that night, not only was the door to Mom and Dad's bedroom shut but the dead babies' doors, as well. Everything was eerily silent, and for a blessed moment, ghostly dust had come to rest.

Dad stayed home from work the next day while I biked to Forest Hill to tune a piano. After I got back, Dad drove to work in mid-afternoon and I crept upstairs to check on Mom. I hated going up there but was thankful that the babies' rooms were quiet and their doors still shut. Mom lay on her side across the bed, eyes closed. *Good,* I thought. *She'll stay like that for a while and I can go out for a bit.*

I left for the cemetery where I wandered among still-flowering trees and bushes, many of them attracting birds and small animals. Listening for songs of the earth and birds,

I also cocked an ear for the movement of leaves and grass and all of their colours. Doing that always helped me deal with my emotions, to cope with whatever was happening at home. I loved the cemetery because it was peaceful, beautiful, and suffused with soft colours. Besides, this graveyard had one of the finest tree collections in North America, with hundreds of varieties, some of them very old.

As I absorbed the sounds and their colours, I wondered again what had attracted my parents to buy a house overlooking a cemetery, a property divided from it only by a wooden fence. Headstones rose at the foot of our house, and a few towered above it. Some people, I knew, would find all this creepy, but not me. And obviously not Mom and Dad.

Yikes! It was after six o'clock, and I'd forgotten about Mom. I climbed a headstone, leaped the fence, and ran along the side of the house to the front.

Uncle Albert's car was parked outside at the curb. My heart sped up with both fright and relief. What if something had happened to Mom while I was out? But thank God I had somebody to talk to. Uncle Albert stood in the doorway surveying the street, deep creases furrowing his brow.

"Julian," he said abruptly, "your mother's not here. Weren't you supposed to be watching her? Where were you, and where do you suppose she's gone?"

"She's not here?" Alarm and guilt widened my eyes, and I couldn't meet his eye. *Damn!* She was wandering off again! "I'm so sorry. I just slipped out for a few minutes because she was sleeping. How long have you been here?" Meaning, how long had she been gone.

"I just got here. Look, you sprint off toward Mount Pleasant. I'll take the car and cruise east to Bayview. We'll give it a half-hour, and if we don't find her, we'll have to call the police."

Not that again! I darted up the sloping street to Mount

Pleasant. Why I chose to go north I had no idea. I sprinted past the Esso gas station, Kentucky Fried Chicken, and other buildings and small shops until I approached the Baptist church and The Longest Yard restaurant on the corner of Belsize Avenue. At first I didn't see anyone but had a hunch about the church. As I hurried toward it, I caught sight of something white flapping in the breeze. *Mom!* She was huddled on the bottom concrete step, head lowered over her folded arms as if she were a homeless waif.

With some struggling, I got Mom back home and into bed. Chastened, despondent, I tried to explain to Uncle Albert, and to Dad who had rushed home from work, what had happened.

"I don't know how she did it!" I cried. "I left her sleeping —"

"Never mind," Dad said. "Go see if there's anything we can eat." He and Uncle Albert went into the dining room and sat on opposite sides of it. As I scrounged in the fridge for leftover food, I glanced up and glimpsed through the doorway their two heads bent low. They had removed their blazers, and their shirts gleamed white in the darkness of the room.

Mom, in a fit of manic energy a few months earlier, had painted the dining room walls entirely black. She'd said at the time, "If a room has very little natural light, you paint it in dark colours and then you're all snug like you're in a cocoon." Right now, in the dim light, my father and uncle seemed like stick figures in urgent dialogue. I stood there full of foreboding. Next thing I imagined seeing the ghosts of my dead siblings sidling along the walls, hearing their cries. Everything made me feel sick, then a hideous thought struck me: maybe I was the one who was crazy.

Mentally, I shook myself. In the pantry, I found cans of tuna, and in the fridge, some mayonnaise and a jar of pickles. Armed with these supplies, I slapped together some sandwiches and took them into the dining room. Then I poured three cups of coffee that had been sitting in the pot since breakfast, but didn't think anyone would care. Dad looked up at me with wet eyes; he'd been crying. Uncle Albert nodded at me, his expression inscrutable. I returned to the kitchen and made myself a sandwich but then didn't feel like eating it. The silence in the dining room while Dad and Uncle Albert ate had a harsh quality to it, even ominous.

"Julian." Uncle Albert's voice startled me. He was standing beside me in the kitchen. "Look, why don't I take you out somewhere and have a talk. Your dad —"

"No!" Dad sat back in his chair, uncharacteristically vehement. "Julian should go see his mother before she's taken to the hospital. He wasn't watching her before, so I think he must do so now. He's her only son, after all."

"Go on, Julian. Go see your mother," Dad repeated. "Impress on her that you're indeed her son. She's going to the Clarke Institute tomorrow, and I don't know when you'll be allowed to see her …" His voice trailed away. The Clarke Institute was a place for mental patients, and fear of what it meant made me shut down my feelings even more.

"We'll have a talk another time, Julian," Uncle Albert said with a tight smile. But he remained standing in the kitchen, staring out the window.

Feeling sick, rebellious, and sorry, I tiptoed upstairs and into my parents' bedroom where Mom lay under a pile of bedclothes. I tried to talk to her, and at one point she turned her head and peered at me.

"It's Julian, Mom, come to see how you are."

"Who are you?"

"Julian," I said, raising my voice. "Your son, Julian."

"No, you're not. Why pretend you are? *My* son, Jeremy, is dead."

I bolted out of the room and back downstairs in a few seconds flat. Uncle Albert took one look at my face and said,

"Come on, kid, let's you and I go out for a drink — yes, you're old enough to have one, and you need it."

We left Dad sitting deep in his armchair, staring blankly at the television, and drove up Mount Pleasant Road to a restaurant Uncle Albert said was usually quiet. He appeared older suddenly, his face jowly and creased. Dark rings encircled his eyes. After we seated ourselves, after he ordered a bottle of white wine and poured us both a glass, he said, "Now look, Jules, I want you to listen carefully to what I'm going to tell you about your mother. We all need to have sympathy for her. I know about the business of the dead babies, what she calls her missing children, and how it must disturb you —"

"Freaks me out is more like it."

"Of course, it would anyone." He drained his glass and poured himself another. "Let me try to explain. When a woman — or a man — loses a baby, either in the womb before they're born, or more usually afterward when something happens to them, it can make them see the world differently, you know, permanently change them. Some parents, like your mother, feel the dead baby's spirit very deeply. Even long after they have a living child, like you, it's like having one child on one side of a divide and the dead child on the other. Your mom has never been able to forget the dead ones, and sometimes she hears them whispering to her. She can't *ever* forget," he repeated with emphasis. "You've suffered the misfortune to have to live under the shadow of a phantom brother and two phantom sisters, to have a mother who knows how easily a heartbeat can stop. The fear of it almost makes her own heart stop. I must also explain this. When your brother and sisters died, your mother just purely and simply wanted to die, too. That's why I ... well, never mind that."

Uncle Albert's face twisted and crumpled up as though he might cry. In his voice, there was the sound and colour of agony, and all I could do was sit there dumbly and stare at him. He rubbed his eyes and continued. "When she saw you were strong and healthy, when she saw she wouldn't lose you, life for her became a confused swirl full of both joy and sorrow. Again, as I said, unfortunately for you, you've always had to live with dead siblings. You must understand how much your mother's heart will always ache for them, as you've seen. But, and this is very important, it doesn't mean she doesn't love —"

"She told me just now that I wasn't her son, that her real son was dead," I interrupted.

Another twist of pain jolted my uncle's face, and I saw tears form in his eyes. Then he straightened in his chair, took his elbows off the table, and put his hands in his lap. "Now listen to me. Whatever your mother said, she didn't mean it. She's not in her right mind. But she'll get better. She won't even remember she said that. It's just now that things are hard for her. For your dad, too." He picked up his glass, drained it, and poured some more wine. This disturbed me, too because I'd never seen him drink.

"Uncle Albert," I said, hearing the urgency in my voice. "Dad said she had a psychotic depression. That's called mental illness, isn't it? Does that kind of thing run in a family? I … you know some of the kids at school call me a nerd, and they probably think I'm a bit weird. And —" I dropped my head "— sometimes I hear the babies cry. When I'm really tired or pissed off, I can even see them — tiny ghosts sliding along the walls of my room. Should I be worried? Am I going crazy, too? Do you think I could have inherited —"

"No!"

I flinched at the vehemence in his voice. Uncle Albert leaned across the table with urgency in his posture. With his face close to mine, eyes intense, he said, "You're different, Julian. Don't ask me to explain right now. Just take it from me — okay?"

When we got home, we found Uncle Robert in the house talking to Dad, the two of them in the living room, Uncle Robert seated in Mom's chair. The vertical blinds on the front windows were closed.

As he always did when he saw me, Uncle Robert looked me up and down, giving me the feeling that he hoped to find me not exactly failing but not doing well, either. I didn't understand his attitude, but the colours attached to it were angry streaks of black and blood-red.

"So, young fellow," his voice boomed around the living room walls, "a little bit of difficulty here with your mother, but you're what, sixteen, seventeen? Nothing you can't handle, eh?"

As always when in his presence, I felt like an object being evaluated, as though I were a foreign creature parachuted into the family. I didn't remember what we said, only that Uncle Albert was abrupt with him and I sensed the tension between them, the violent purple colours attached to it. Uncle Robert then shrugged and left not long after.

CHAPTER TWELVE

Mom was in the hospital for three weeks. When she returned home, a nurse dropped in every day to check on her and make sure she took her medication. Once a week, Dad took her to the Clarke Institute to see her psychiatrist.

Through all the events at home, thoughts and images of Louisa were my salvation. In my mind, I saw an angelic figure hovering around me, smiling and laughing her rippling laugh. Her voice thrummed in my head. Then, with my heart speeding up, I'd get on my bike and hurtle through the streets of North Toronto, counting the minutes until school started. School meant Louisa. She had been up north most of the summer but was surely home now. I thought about riding past her house to catch a glimpse of her but then figured that wasn't a good idea, so I began repeating her name under my breath instead.

One day I parked my bike outside the small library on the east side of Mount Pleasant Road, went in, and perused the books being promoted before heading for the classics section. We'd studied Thomas Hardy's *Tess of the d'Urbervilles* in Grade 11, but I wanted to read it again, to immerse myself in the idealistic, fatalistic love Angel had for Tess. I also wanted to find and read some of the world's great love stories, hoping they'd validate mine, help me to understand it. I was in love and felt rich and alive, like somebody else, not me at all. With my eyes ranging over titles in the classics section, I tried to recall some of the books Mom had read before she'd gotten hooked on modern-day romances. This gave me pause, and I wondered for the first time what had brought about the change in her reading habits. I expected that because they were incremental I'd never be able to sort out when things for her began to change.

I remembered some of the characters of the books that had lain around the house. There was Heloise ... Heloise and who? Yes, Peter Abelard and Heloise, an unlikely couple who suffered horribly for their love. Dimly, I remembered that Abelard was castrated and eventually became a monk. Heloise confined herself to a nunnery. But the flame of their urgent love never dimmed.

There was someone else Mom used to read. As I rifled through my mind, eventually it came to me — the eighteenth-century poet Novalis or Fritz von Hardenberg, who had fallen in love with a plain-looking, uneducated fifteen-year-old girl. Tragically, she died not long after the two became engaged, and he followed her into the grave not many years afterward.

I leaned against one end of a bookcase, these historical figures scuttling through my mind. Once I'd tried to explain some of what I felt about Louisa to Jack, but he'd poked me in the ribs and said, "Come on, Jules, you're not in love. All you want is to get into her pants. I mean, that's all most guys ever want. You think you're any different? It's the girls who do the swooning stuff. That Louisa? I bet all she wants is to get into *your* pants."

An image of Louisa naked flashed before me, and my blood ran hot in my veins. At that moment, I thought Jack was wrong. Louisa was the personification of all that was pure and beautiful, and my feelings for her were as chaste as for any angelic creature. Behind me I heard my name, spoken in a voice similar to Louisa's, and I jumped.

"Julian." Pam Blackstock was standing beside me, smiling, arms, as always, full of books.

"Oh, hi, you startled me." I knew my grin was forced, maybe even goofy. "What are all those books? School hasn't even started." I felt awkward. I knew how she felt about Louisa, knew how she treated her — if what Louisa had said was true.

Pam stood closer to me, invading my body buffer zone. I stepped away, but then she put a hand on my shoulder and suggested we go somewhere, maybe to Penrose to buy a Coke and a basketful of chips.

Whoa! Was she asking me to go on a date? I *could* like her, I supposed. I *would* like her, but only if Louisa didn't exist. I ended up mumbling no, that I had to get home, got on my bike, and feeling both confused and elated, pedalled furiously to Robbie's house, hoping to find him there so I could ask him what he thought.

CHAPTER THIRTEEN

I knew Grade 12 would be loaded with homework, tests, exams, and studying hard to improve my marks. I'd have to make momentous decisions about the future — college, university, maybe the trades. I knew all that, but my mind remained dizzy with thoughts and visions of Louisa.

As I dawdled up Mount Pleasant that first day of school, I felt the weight of the deciduous trees still carrying their burden of leaves, a natural world poised to put a bright face on approaching death. At school I resumed my spot near the old pine tree, sometimes sitting on one of the great slabs of granite leading to its Gothic entrance. I felt edgy, excited. I strained to see through the knots of students, to listen for the sound of Louisa's voice, her laugh. I waited. My longing turned slowly to fear that she wouldn't show up. To distract myself, I tilted my head to listen for the songs of trees, bushes, birds, and dying flowers. Still no sign of Louisa, and my anxiety melded with the sounds of the natural world. E flat became D sharp. E sharp became F natural — same thing really. I was so involved in identifying the different keys for the various sounds that I almost missed Louisa's advent. I used the word *advent* deliberatively, for wherever she was she created a happening. First, I glimpsed the red-and-black scarf. Then I heard the quick, short footsteps, and there she was, surging along the school's entranceway, short skirt flying around her thighs. I raced after her, my heart beating furiously, joyously.

"Lou!" I cried out.

"Louisa." The reply was automatic. She turned, gave me what I called her non-personal smile, and said, "Hi again. A good summer? God, can you stand another year of school?" And she disappeared inside the school.

"Wait ... wait!" What had just happened? Breath stopped in my lungs, and I felt I'd just been erased. I was stunned, not believing she'd blown me off like that.

I scarcely listened to anything that was said in classes that day and quickly returned to my old habits. I loitered in hallways, in classrooms, on the street, hoping to catch a glimpse of my idol, to pick up the sound of her voice. One day, not seeing her anywhere outdoors, I hung around inside the main hall, my eyes running over the lists of names of Northern Secondary's graduate students who had died in the Second World War.

"You getting hung up on dead people?" Robbie asked, standing alongside me.

"I ... what?"

"Those guys have been dead a long time. Same as the ones in the cemetery, and that's where you're always hanging around."

"What?" I asked again, then seeing the teasing look in his eyes, punched his shoulder. Together we walked out the door.

"Forget Louisa," Robbie said. "Let's go to your place and look at that thing you're building in the basement."

"That thing" was my attempt to build a raft that would float. I longed to show it to him, to have him help me with it, but didn't want him to have to make conversation with Mom and see how crazy she was. As I walked home that afternoon,

I remembered how Robbie had said, "Forget Louisa." He might as well have told me to forget that *I* existed.

Early mornings saw me maintaining my old habits: leaning against the old pine tree, perching on one of the granite boulders, watching and waiting for Louisa. Once I caught a glimpse of Steve surrounded by Leon and his coterie. *What's he doing with them?* Then I forgot him and dragged myself at the last minute into the school's hallowed halls. What I needed, I thought, was another chance to slay Leon and rescue Louisa from his ugly paws.

At mid-morning break, suddenly there she was, swinging alongside Leon in the hallway. I stared. Something shifted. A peculiar sensation wrapped itself around me, and I felt as if the boundaries of myself were dissolving, that all at once I existed everywhere and nowhere. People merged into one another. I panicked, thinking I must have inherited some mental illness from Mom. But as they usually did, voices from the past saved me.

Uncle Albert's voice: "Math, my boy, you're good already, but you can be better. Math is where the future is."

Dad's voice: "Think accountancy, Jules, even actuarial science."

Mom's voice: "You're good at most things, dear Julian."

As Louisa and Leon disappeared from my sight, my mind lingered on images of Mom, how more recently when she saw me, she nodded and smiled at me — a bit vacantly, I thought. She had been home from hospital for about ten days, and though still sedated, she was definitely making progress.

To escape my misery about Louisa's brush-off, I turned my mind to Uncle Albert, willing his voice to come to me again. It fell softly upon me, like balm applied to a bruise. "You know how it's said that math and music go together, but do you know why? I'm not thinking of algebra, geometry, physics, calculus, and other sorts, but pure arithmetic …" As I listened to his voice in my head, I summoned images of him, and soon his eyes were on me, intense, probing, concentrating on what he supposed he saw in me, listening the way few people do to others. The warmth of it all but overwhelmed me, and I remembered how once I'd rushed to give him a hug.

"Well, now, my boy, what's all this about?" He clapped a hand on my shoulder but immediately turned away and said he had places to be. Perhaps he was embarrassed about my show of affection.

Upset with myself, having a powerful wish to please him, I'd made a decision to pursue math to the best of my ability. I would do it also because I had a feel for it and enjoyed it. Unlike so much else in life — in my life — math offered clear premises and deductive reasoning. It had strict boundaries, was unambiguous, and led to exact answers.

Slowly, the boundaries of myself came back together as images of Louisa, arm in arm with Leon, slowly faded.

CHAPTER FOURTEEN

In the second half of Grade 12, nothing really changed with Louisa, not even after what I supposed had been my privileged intimacy with her previously. I became vaguely aware of somebody following me. Who? And why? I began glancing quickly over my shoulder, suddenly spinning around. Twice I thought I spotted a figure disappearing around a corner, a shadowy presence behind a tree. But I dismissed it and maintained my lonely vigil near the school entrance.

Into those elegant but musty school halls of oak and maple wood, adolescents of all ages and sizes clattered. Among the clamour of voices of today, ghosts of other ages floated, intertwined with Louisa's voice, her laugh everywhere. I followed the sounds of it, lost it, picked it up again, ran after her, then at the last minute, turned away.

Winter persisted into early March, then passed messily into spring. In the cool air, Louisa wore a puffy jacket and skimpy dress that revealed pale, freckled legs. A few freckles also dotted her nose. Her eyes were black-rimmed and fluttery as before. Occasionally, as she walked away on dates with other guys, she rested those eyes on me with an expression I couldn't decipher. Of course, I'd dreaded she would lose interest in me after that summer break, but it hurt more than anything I could ever have imagined, worse than the worst toothache. Another heroic rescue was needed, and all the while I worked and studied hard, watched and waited.

Then came the evening of the semi-formal school year-end graduation dance where lineups for Louisa snaked around the perimeter of the gymnasium. I flattened myself against a wall, eyes darting around the cavernous room in search of her, a room of stained concrete, defaced walls, and a floor leaking sweaty smells. But tonight it became a moving, perfumed garden of giddy girls, flowers the colours of earth, sky, and thunderstorms. A few girls wore black, and I supposed they felt sophisticated.

Someone squeezed alongside me, invading my space — I was particular about that — and then others until I felt I was invisible, that I didn't even exist. What the hell!

Another person shoved past me and pushed his way into the centre of the gym — Leon! Privately, I called him "The Indomitable," since he cowed most other kids who, for self-protection, gave him grudging respect. At this moment he continued to elbow his way among the thickening crowd. With curiosity I watched to see who he wanted tonight, since it wasn't always Louisa he was after. As I studied him, I thought how paradoxical it was that together with a mean, bullying personality, physically he was good-looking: a round face, high cheekbones, wide brown eyes, long lashes, and a full mouth. Then I wondered about the influences that had formed him into the person he was, but I knew little about his background.

Ah, he's going after Louisa! I watched as he pushed his way through a knot of students surrounding her. Did he just want to show off that he could get her, or did he really want her? She dodged him, playing games with him, I thought, remembering how recently she had gone off arm in arm with him. Then he grasped one of her arms with a meaty hand and with his other swiped at anyone who tried to steer him away. Louisa swore at him and managed to yank herself free. Blood rushed to Leon's face but again he thrust himself at her. Grabbing a handful of her hair, he hauled her toward the door.

"You're a flirt, a slut!" he yelled, his voice bouncing off the dirty grey walls. "You give yourself to these idiot guys, so you'll give it to me, too." With a hand now firmly clutching her, he pulled her in the direction of the gymnasium door. Many of the other boys fell away in awe of remembered defeat at his hands.

"Get your grubby paws off me!" Louisa's voice had risen to a shout. She swore, and at her language, I blushed to the roots of my flat fair hair. In an instant, her usual pose of fragility became a fierce windmilling of arms and legs. Dancers scattered to the perimeter of the gym, and I speculated if I was the only one who had picked up the rumble of menace bubbling beneath the sudden silence in the room. Uneasy, I cast around for any of the teachers who had organized the event, who were supposed to be monitoring this affair and intervene at signs of trouble, but I saw no one.

I doubted Leon had seen me. If he had, he might have remembered his previous humiliation at my hands and would think for a moment about what he was doing. Hatred for him raced through me like poison, and wanting to protect Louisa, I lunged at him, my right fist smashing into his face. As before, Leon ended up on the floor with a bloodied nose and cut lower lip.

I stood over him, our eyes locking. In mine he must have seen the astonishment I felt. In his there was a fury that made me quickly step away from him, even while he remained on the floor.

"Julian!"

I turned. Mr. Agnew, the history teacher, stood beside me, a surprised expression on his face. He glanced down at Leon, then back at me. "It would be better if you settled your differences outside school. Bending to Leon, he asked, "Are you okay?" Without waiting for an answer, he walked away.

Afterward, I knew my second success against Leon was a fluke, powered by my belief that a man should do everything he could to protect a woman, any woman, but especially this one.

Louisa's eyes, huge and fluttery, were on me. A small smile turned up the corners of her lips. In response, I put my head down and walked away. After that she hung around me, her eyes full of curiosity about me. She waited for me after classes, and if she caught up with me, she chatted non-stop about her teachers, her dumb classmates, her horrible sister, Pam. She asked me where I was going after school, would I help her with math and science, would I escort her home.

"You know you're a strange one," she said one late afternoon as we strolled south on Mount Pleasant. "None of the other guys would ever dare take on Leon. Why did you? He could have killed you, you know."

Feeling colour rise in my face — how I hated that! — I asked, "Why do you go out with him, why make eyes at him, then turn him away?"

"Are you defending him?"

"N-no, I'm just saying that what you do might confuse him."

"Well, then, how about I make eyes at you instead?" Louisa batted her eyelashes and turned in a circle while tossing her hair.

Don't do that! I wanted to yell at her. *Don't you remember last summer? You were a different person then. It's me, Julian, you're talking to.* Of course, I didn't say any of that. Vaguely, I registered that the short tight skirts she'd worn were now replaced by skinny jeans with holes in the knees. Her hair was growing long. For days and weeks, a war had raged in my head and heart. My head said: "You're just another fellow for her to conquer, a bit different from the rest who only want one thing. Right now she's romanticizing you, the big man who arrived in time to save the little maid. Soon enough your big hero image will wear off just like before." My heart said: "She's like a river, always shifting and changing shape. She glitters over the earth and everything in it. She's vibrant, exciting, and I want it. I want *her*."

CHAPTER FIFTEEN

"Jules, will you walk home with me?" Louisa's voice was a golden halo all around me.

"Of course, if you want me to." My own voice came out breathless. Heat rose in my neck to my ears. I'd just finished a music lesson with Mr. Jeffreys when Louisa sprinted down the hallway toward me.

We set off south to Eglinton, heading west toward Hillsdale, the world so lit up for me that I felt it could scorch my eyeballs. The late-afternoon sun hung low as a shadow, not ours, moved, and I realized that someone's footsteps were keeping pace with ours. "Stop. Wait." I spun around. "I saw a shadow move!"

Louisa laughed. "Jules, you're seeing things."

The footsteps quickened, and the shadow slid away, but not before I recognized the bulky form of Steve, the particular slope of his shoulders, head squat on his short neck. "I'm sure that was my cousin. Lately, I've had a weird feeling someone was following me. But why on earth?" Was I beginning to imagine Steve was morphing into a phantom like the babies at home?

"If it's him, he's the one with a problem," Louisa said. "Forget him."

A brisk wind blew old leaves and papers around, and we kicked at them. Louisa bobbed along beside me, chattering about school, teachers, and exams. But a tight feeling had fallen across my shoulders. Why was Steve following me, supposing it had been him? Also, I felt weighed down with anxiety that I might not be able to match Louisa's mood, to keep up with her conversation, to be witty, amusing, and intelligent in the way I envisaged she liked. My joy, and my burden, was to keep her desiring me.

Damn him! Why is he hanging around us? The figure I'd thought was Steve reappeared a few moments later, advancing toward us. Grabbing Louisa's arm, I whispered, "Let's go the other way." But Steve kept coming, and my feet remained stuck to the pavement. When he was level with us, he stopped and raked his eyes over us as though to absorb every detail. Then he walked right past without saying a word.

I looked after his retreating figure with foreboding. Steve's eyes were sunken, dull, his face thinner, the rest of his body, too. He appeared haunted.

"What was that all about?" I asked the empty street.

"Hey, forget him." Louisa said, chasing away my lingering bad feeling. She skipped ahead of me, then ran back and looped her arm through mine. Arm in arm, we turned up Manor Road instead of continuing to Hillsdale.

"Here," Louisa said, "It's private behind the church."

It was. We flopped onto the grass outside the Church of the Transfiguration. *Beautiful*, I thought, my eyes roving over its pretty grey stone walls half covered in climbing ivy, a sanctuary in the midst of the clamour, noise, and frenzy of life. We ambled over knolls and along walkways to find a spot in long summer grass. Before I flopped onto my back, I searched for lurking figures and moving shadows, but there were none ... nothing. I released a long breath and lay down to study a pale blue sky etched with scrolls of shifting clouds.

The next minute Louisa was on top of me, her heavily pencilled eyes peering straight into mine. Alarmed — we were in a public place, after all — I pushed her off and sat up. "People will see us," I said, frowning and laughing at the same time. She giggled as she edged back up beside me. Still fluttering her eyes, twisting a strand of her hair in her fingers, she leaned over me again, face close to mine.

I twisted away from her, and with a sense of urgency, said, "Look, Lou —"

"Louisa."

"Sorry. Louisa, we can't just —"

"You know, you're a lonesome fellow, aren't you?" She sat back on her heels, curiosity reflected in her face. "I mean, I know you have a couple of nerdy friends, but do you have any relatives at all other than your parents and Uncle Albert?"

Surprised at the comment, I said, "Well, not many. Besides Uncle Albert, I've got one other aunt and uncle, and one cousin."

"Okay. Where are they?"

"They moved to Niagara Falls."

"Do you ever see them?"

I smiled. "You're quite the inquisitor, aren't you? Hardly ever. They don't seem to get along too well with my parents, and there's something odd about Steve, that guy who passed us on the street. No one ever mentions him, as though he's got some dreadful disease or because he's a bit batty. Maybe he's murdered someone."

I'd said all that lightly, but as I'd done so, Steve's face had floated before me, followed by Leon's scowling visage. Leon. Steve. A burst of clarity fell over me. Drugs. That was it! Steve was into drugs. I couldn't explain why I thought this, but right now I felt it to be true. It certainly accounted for the silences around him, his physical absence from our family. *Do you want to be one of the big boys?* he once asked me, and I hadn't clued in at the time that he was referring to drugs.

"I'd love to go to Niagara Falls," Louisa said. "I've never been." She propped herself on one elbow and lay there with her eyes half closed. "We all begged Mom and Dad to take us once, but they said there were too many of us to manage and it was way too expensive to get us all there. We'd want rides and things they couldn't afford."

Suddenly, she sat back up on her heels. Her eyes sparking, mouth twitching, she added, "Jules, you could take me, couldn't you? You could borrow your father's car and we could drive there and back in one day. Couldn't you? *Couldn't you?* Do they live close to the Falls? Can you see them from their house?"

"No and no," I said, not taking her seriously. "They live on Barclay Street in the northwest part of the city and would have to take a bus to get to the Falls."

"Steve ... what's his last name?"

"Why do you want to know? Same as mine — Whitely."

I saw how she absorbed this, noticed her staring into space. Minutes passed. Louisa picked at the cuticles on her fingers. As before, I felt she'd suddenly lost interest in me and in what we were talking about until she turned back, and laughing, said, "Hey, you and I make quite a pair. Julian Whitely, shining white knight. Louisa Blackstock, black sheep of the family."

"Ha. I have to disagree. The name Blackstock has more solidity to it. Listen, on a completely different subject, there's something I want to ask you." I sat up and brushed dry grass off me.

"Okay, ask me anything, lover boy."

"It's just that ... what you're doing now ... I mean, why do you do that with your eyes — you know how you do — and persuade all the boys to fall in love with you? You've got them fighting over you. It's not fair to them, and as for me, well, I really don't know what you want."

"Don't you, big boy?" She leaned across the space between us and planted a lingering kiss on my lips before flopping onto her back on the grass. "Julian, do you like me?" Her eyes seemed to pop right out of her face. The heels of her boots tapped on the grass with an impatient, or perhaps, anxious rhythm, I wasn't sure.

"Of course, I do. What's not to like?" But I'd said that too quickly.

"You don't go after me. You don't want me to do things like other guys."

I didn't want to imagine what things other guys might do, so I asked, "Why do you like *me* when you can have any fellow?"

"Oh, that's easy. You're *nice*. You're the only honest guy in the whole school, the most interesting by light years. You … you're *deep*."

Her words felt fresh and sincere.

"I like your big, good-humoured face, and hey, wait. I'm going to kiss it again." With traffic roaring alongside us, with the sniggering of kids in the distance, she grasped my arms, pulled me toward her, and kissed my lips. "I want to come to your house."

CHAPTER SIXTEEN

I want to come to your house. I was on the grass with Louisa tickling me, planting little kisses all over my face, when suddenly a voice called out, "Lou! I know you're there! Mom wants you. She said you're to come right away."

Louisa swore under her breath. "It's my little sister, Bunny," she whispered in my ear. "I wonder if she's been following us. If she has, I'll spit on her!"

"*Shhh*," I said, astonished at her language.

"I bet Mom doesn't want me. Bunny's making it up. She's into everything these days. It's really annoying." But Louisa scrambled to her feet and brushed herself down. "You stay here. Don't move. Maybe Bunny hasn't seen you, after all." Next thing she was gone.

It might not have been Mrs. Blackstock's intention to thwart further development of my relationship with Louisa, but that early summer she found many responsibilities for her daughter. To look after her younger siblings. To be tutored in math in the evenings, since math was her worst subject. To attend Camp Elizabeth up north for the whole of August.

Absence made the heart grow fonder, it was said, and the obstacles thrown up did indeed increase our desire to be with each other. I suppose I should have spoken for myself, since I could never be sure of Louisa. Only much later did I wonder — a depressing thought — that for her, her attempts to communicate with me might have been more the excitement of outwitting her mother than her wish to be with me.

After I graduated from high school, I worked with Uncle Albert tuning pianos, practising scales, perfecting my playing of "Humoresque." All the while I saved up for the tuition costs of getting an accountancy certificate. Every Saturday I took piano lessons with old Mr. Jeffreys, the school music teacher. Without Louisa dancing around me teasing and laughing, I felt my life plodding, even boring, that I was without much substance except for one thing — my burgeoning love affair with the piano. The chords I played summoned colours. They altered my mood and even the ambience in our house. Then there was Mom. I always knew when a bout of depression was about to descend on her.

"Jules dear boy," she'd say, her crocheting needle still in her lap, "please play me some of those nice pieces I hear you practise downstairs — that composer you like, Schumann, isn't it?"

I played the composer's *Childhood Fantasies*, and Clara Schumann's *Romances*, over and over. I kept playing as Mom wandered the house restlessly, as she slumped in a chair by the piano and closed her eyes. While my fingers danced over the keys, I took fleeting glances and saw the lines on her face soften, her colour return. Throughout the night, I played for her, first, Borodin's "Nocturne," then Debussy's "Clair de lune." I thought that as long as I did so, she wouldn't get worse. She might even get better. My shoulders ached, my fingers all but bled, but I played until the hazy light of dawn crept through the basement's small window.

But Mom only got worse. That summer she got so bad that she was briefly hospitalized a second time.

During the days I played for Mom, some part of my brain held on to dreams of Louisa, a lifesaving antidote to the darkness that settled over our house. On late afternoons, I lay on the grass in the cemetery and conjured her in the wildest of colours until my eyelids burned. I fashioned images of her floating high above the dreariness and sameness of my brain like silvery moonbeams. Louisa was the perfection of all that was beautiful, sweet, and innocent. One day ... one day ... she would be mine! I could hardly breathe.

As that summer drew softly to its close, as Mom improved, I turned all my thoughts to Louisa. Anxiety built as I remembered the blow-off she'd given me the summer in high school when I hadn't seen her for two months.

On August 30 came a breathless phone call. "Hey-ho, Jules! I gotta see you! Meet me outside The Longest Yard — soon, right now!"

Joyous summons indeed!

"My mom needs me," I said to Mr. Jeffreys on the phone right before a piano lesson. "I'm afraid I'll have to skip my lesson. So sorry for the short notice. I'll be sure to practise Bach before I come next week."

I ran out of the house and all the way up Mount Pleasant Road to Belsize. There, in shadows cast by the restaurant's patio awning, stood Louisa, and next thing I knew, suntanned arms were thrown around me, bleached hair blew in my face, kisses rained over me.

"I'm coming to your house," Louisa announced. "I should meet your mother. I think we should tell your parents we're getting engaged." There was a wild energy about her, a kind of recklessness.

"*Engaged?*" My heart seemed to stop and fly into my throat, the wretched crimson no doubt rising in my face. "Lou ... Louisa, we're hardly out of high school and we've never talked about that ..."

"Hey, big boy, we don't have to do it today." Louisa's teasing voice swirled around me, and laughing, she pulled on my earlobes. "Come on, at least let me meet your mother."

Even though Mom had been pretty good lately, I worried how she'd react to the idea of my getting engaged. I tried to put Louisa off.

"What?" she said. "You got some skeletons hidden away, maybe a few ghosts?" Then she saw my face. "Whoa, lighten up. I'm just kidding."

And so one bright Sunday afternoon we swung down the road and along Merton Street to number 107.

I glanced sideways at Louisa as we walked and whistled. "Hey, do you plan to give Mom a heart attack? She's never seen a girl like you." I let my eyes rove over Louisa's makeup and her way-out clothes.

"Well, surely, you've brought girls home before?"

"Not like you." I chose not to confess she was the very first. But immediately I forgot about that, forgot about the phantom babies, concerned only about how Mom would act around my girlfriend. I wondered if I should warn Louisa that my Mom was sometimes a bit odd, but decided against it. If Mom behaved erratically, I'd say she was depressed and leave it at that.

As we strolled, I cocked my head to listen for the different songs of birds as I habitually did until Louisa asked, "Jules, what are you doing? You're not even looking where you're going. Open your eyes, see what you're missing." Her hands fluttered in the air, pointing. "See? This little flower shop, this pub. Look at this store called George's Trains. Tennis courts over there — have you ever played on them? That Baptist church — I wonder how people go to it. Have you ever been in a church? You're lucky to have the park on your doorstep — or maybe not."

"Hey," I said, "give me that hand or you'll knock off my nose with it." I felt the snap in my step, felt myself rich, powerful, omniscient. "See? I do look and notice things. See what you missed — Kentucky Fried Chicken? Let's stop for something to eat and drink." And so we sat on the curb gobbling fries and sipping Cokes in the dusty late-afternoon sun as traffic roared by on its way out of the city.

Louisa glanced up and down Merton Street. I looked through her eyes, seeing it as though for the first time: smallish square and oblong red-brick houses, for the most part. Some were detached, but most were semis or row houses. Tidy front gardens clashed with neglected ones. When we finished our snack and continued on, I pointed to our house as we neared it: a semi-detached with a neat front garden where the heads of irises and bright yellow gladiolas nodded in the late-summer breeze.

Out of the blue, Louisa said, "You're lucky to have your parents all to yourself, you know. Like, no competition, no lining up for the bathroom, no arguing about who gets to sit at the table and have second helpings."

She had mentioned this once before, but now I began to understand her vulnerability, the fear she'd be forgotten or overlooked among seven children. Later still came the realization that most of what she did was for this purpose: getting noticed, to know she was okay, that she was pretty, desirable. *That* was why she enticed boys, and thinking this, I excused all her flirtatious behaviour.

"Honestly, I really can't imagine it," I said now. "I'd give anything to have a big family and not to be the only one. Being an only child, it's awful. Everything's piled on you and you have to carry all your parents' expectations. Come and see for yourself." But doubt suddenly entered my mind and I added, "If Mom acts a bit funny, just ignore it. She's been sick, you know, a bit depressed, but she's getting over it."

My mother wore a light blue skirt with a cream blouse and pearls. She'd washed and set her hair so that it bounced in little curls around her face, and she had blush on her cheeks and pink lipstick.

Pleased at this, and with a good feeling, I made the introductions. Mom considered Louisa with sharp eyes, from the purple-streaked hair cut in sharp geometric lines, to her jaunty tank top, to the tight jean skirt stretching across her bum to barely cover it. Shiny black boots rose almost to her knees. When at last Mom raised her eyes, it was to stare hard into Louisa's black-pencilled ones. Hers narrowed, her pink lips thinned, and she withdrew the faint smile she'd offered. Standing straight in front of the living room mantel, she folded her arms across her breasts.

Dad appeared in the living room doorway then, looking surprised, then brightening. With Mom's eyes on him, he mumbled about being glad to meet his son's new friend, dropped his eyes to the floor, and backed out of the room.

Louisa strode around the living room, taking note of every knick-knack, photo, print on the walls. She took in the maroon mats scattered on the hardwood floors, the vertical blinds at the windows, the flowered cushions on the couch and armchairs.

"Ugh, what's with the black walls?" she exclaimed as she stood in the doorway to the dining room.

"Mom thinks it makes a room without any natural light warm and cozy," I said. "That was the idea, wasn't it, Mom? So now that you've done your once-over of our house, Louisa, let me show you the backyard." What I meant was: *Let's get away from Mom.*

"First, you should offer your guest some tea," Mom said, still standing by the mantel.

I noted her use of the word *guest*. Not *girlfriend*, not even *friend*.

"Thank you, but I don't need tea," Louisa said. "Mrs. Whitely, from what I can see, you have a very nice house. Do you mind if I see the upstairs, too? Jules, why don't you take me up and show me your room?" She had her foot on the first step before I could grab her arm and make some excuse why she shouldn't. Next thing I knew she was on the top landing, calling to me. "Come on. Show me around up here, Jules."

I glanced at Mom, but her expression was calm. Life was normal. Upstairs was normal. The babies' doors would be closed. As I climbed the stairs, I noticed Mom move from the mantel, pick up her crocheting, and sit down again, fingers busy as though she'd already forgotten we were there.

Damn it all! For the first time, I felt irritated with Louisa. I ran up the remaining steps after her, praying that my phantom sisters' bedroom door was closed.

No such luck! We walked past the open door of the bedroom where baby smells drifted, where lavender perfumed the air. Louisa studied my dead sisters' room, the empty cots, framed baby faces, toys heaped on dressers, dolls, music boxes, baby clothes. I stood beside her, balling my fists. Knots formed in my shoulders, and an ache crept over my forehead. I felt both angry at her ... and embarrassed.

Slowly, Louisa turned and stared at me, eyes large in her face. As though to echo Uncle Albert, she exclaimed, "What the hell, Julian? What's going on?"

"You insisted on seeing the whole house!" I heard anger in my voice. "Why did you have to come nosing up here? Now you're going to listen to something I'll bet you wished you didn't have to. Let's get out of here and I'll explain."

"Wait!" Louisa spun on one foot and started laughing. Slapping me on the shoulder, still laughing, she said, "Well, Julian, I always thought you were deep. An only child, you told me? And all this time you've had two sisters up here! What a dark horse you are!" She seemed excited.

"They've got nothing to do with me!" I protested desperately.

I must have looked so stricken that she took my arm and

said, "Hey, lighten up. People can do what they like and it's nobody's business. You've got a very interesting family."

Back in the living room among the stiff furniture and polished floors, Louisa smiled at my mother and chatted about how nice our house and decorations were, as though they were part of a perfectly normal home. Then, out of the blue, in her prettiest voice, she announced that one day we were going to get engaged, maybe the next year or the one after that. We were young and free. We were getting ourselves educated, and the whole world was out there.

Even though Louisa had just introduced the idea, my mouth gaped at the bold reality of it, at the word *engaged*. Briefly, I wondered if she'd said this for its shock value. Ignoring that thought, I jumped in and said, "And one day we'll have heaps of kids." A huge surge of emotion swelled within me.

"Oh, really?" Surprise flickered on Louisa's face. "Actually, we didn't talk about that. But —" she looked hard at me "— aren't you used to having space and peace and quiet? You have most of your upstairs to yourself."

So she hadn't forgotten my phantom sisters. "No," I said, blithely unaware of a subtle change in her. "I want heaps of kids, and noise and mess and squabbling and laughing and tears — all of it, everywhere, all the time, just like in your house." Another surge of emotion flooded me.

"Not like what's in my house!" After that angry outburst, Louisa lowered her voice and added, "Well, whatever you want, of course, I want, too."

Louisa's voice was flat, but it was lost on me because I'd caught sight of Mom's face: cold, hard, and full of pain. Then, quickly, her expression closed off as she disappeared into her private world.

∞

"Have you forgotten?" Mom demanded after Louisa had floated off into the evening gloom. "You can't have kids, Julian. She'll want them. All women do." Her voice was hollow, her cheeks flat. "I'm sorry, but I don't like her. She's much too flyaway, and you'll never quite know where you are with her. You can do much better." She fiddled with her apron, moved things around on the counter, but I knew she wasn't finished. "Anyway, both of you are much too young. You should think carefully, very carefully, before you go running off to be engaged and married."

"It won't be for years yet," I said.

"You should listen to your mother, Julian," Dad said suddenly.

I jumped. He must have come in without my noticing, and now stood leaning against the living room door, a cup of coffee in one hand, a piece of cake Mom had baked in honour of Louisa's visit in the other.

"What your mother's really trying to say is that the person you marry when you're young is usually not the person you really should. Don't look at us. We got lucky the first time, eh, Muriel?" But his expression conveyed the opposite. "If you go for a second marriage when you're older, or if you wait until you've been around a while and then marry, it's usually, I say, *usually*, to a much more suitable person. Best to grow up some more first."

That was a long speech for Dad, and I gaped at him in surprise. He'd really meant what he'd just said, and I found myself feeling deeply for him. He'd been living with my mother — stuck with her — all these twenty something years, patient, kind, supportive, never complaining.

"Kids, Julian, it's about kids," Mom repeated. "She's very young. She'll want them …"

Kids! Damn it all! The bottom of my world slid from beneath my feet. I hadn't given it a thought, and Louisa and

I hadn't talked about it when we made vague but fanciful plans to be together. We hadn't even actually talked about being engaged; it was just another flight of fancy on her part. *Anyway*, I thought, *why would we talk about having kids at our young ages?*

"She doesn't look like she'll be a good mother." Mom added this as I stood stupefied in the hallway, Louisa now a distant figure along the street. She'd left in a hurry because she couldn't wait to get away from our house. Thinking this, a wave of panic swept over me. Still, she'd laughed about the situation upstairs. Confused, unhappy, I stood next to the living room window, arms hanging at my sides, still captive to Mom's tirade.

"She'll want kids," Mom repeated once more, and as she said that, I glimpsed a great sadness fall over her as her whole face sagged. "You'll have to tell her. It's only fair." But the last words were said with an edge of triumph, which told me how little Mom liked the girl I'd chosen to be with.

Forgetting the "kids" part, I struggled to explain Louisa to Mom. "She says how she hates being in a large family. She wishes she were an only child. But I'm sure she doesn't mean it. She's told me all about the pillow fights, the games, the ganging up, the dressing up."

We'd moved from the living room into the kitchen. Mom fiddled with teacups we hadn't used, picked up a dishcloth, swiped it over the counter, flicked imaginary specks from her blouse.

"Louisa gets all the hand-me-down clothes," I persisted. "No one notices her, and she says it feels like she's not there ... that if she were an only child she'd get all the attention, or at least some."

"Ha! You think that explains her?"

To myself I argued every side, every scenario I could imagine. If Louisa really loved me, she wouldn't care if we couldn't have kids. If we did want them, we could adopt. But what if she pretended she didn't want any? It would mean she really loved me more than anything, more than — But I struggled to pinpoint what else she could love any better, any more.

"Whatever she says now, she'll live to regret it," Mom said, as if to put an end to our conversation about Louisa. "Then it will be too late for her to change her mind. She'll be too old to have them."

CHAPTER SEVENTEEN

Over the months, I learned to tune Mom out as I became more confident of the future. Well established now with Uncle Albert as an instrument maker and piano tuner, I also intended to pursue a certificate in chartered accountancy. And one day, Louisa and I would get ... *engaged*. Mentally, I spun somersaults at the very word. Louisa had her plans, too, enrolling in a makeup artist program at George Brown College's professional beauty school. So what now?

I remained deeply infatuated, in love — who could tell what it was? Nothing existed in the world for me except my idea of Louisa, a girl sublime, beautiful, exotic, the two of us a single unit. I told myself this as I held her off physically, as she teased and pulled at my clothes on the few nights we were alone at my house.

"That's the only reason she goes for you," Robbie said to me. We were leaning against the wall of Ted's Soda, the late-afternoon sun casting checkered shadows across the sidewalk. Robbie, at my height, sized me up and down, a sour expression settled on his face. "It's because you play hard to get."

"She likes me because I'm *nice*," I objected, subconsciously echoing something Louisa had said to me. Robbie should have known that I didn't play games and that I was just a quiet, geeky, don't-look-at-me kind of guy.

But Robbie didn't intend to leave this alone. Still pressed against the wall, he said, "Really, though, Jules, what do the two of you talk about? Do you have anything at all in common? Her sister, Pam, is much more your type."

Pam — the older sister I'd once dubbed The Shepherdess. I remembered her warning but brushed it way. Glaring at Robbie, I was suddenly without words. A dull silence stretched between us until I said, "Well, Louisa tells me about her family. About how she's going to pursue an arts degree because she's interested in design — you know, in making things beautiful."

Robbie shook his head. "The only thing she cares about is making herself beautiful. But forget I said that. What do *you* tell her?"

He wanted to know if I'd told Louisa about Mom and the babies. Ignoring his comments about Louisa, I said, "I tell her about my music, about how I work with numbers —"

"*Numbers?*"

"Yes, numbers." I heard defensiveness in my voice. "Numbers are clean and clear. You deal with them and they're done. No shades of grey to bother about, no unfinished business to haunt you long after. They're all about harmony and order."

As I said that to Robbie, I recalled the conversation I'd had with Louisa and how she'd said, "But numbers are cold and hard. They've got no feelings. They don't mean anything."

"You think they mean *nothing*?" I'd argued. "They can mean people's lives. They can determine where they live, what they do, even what they eat. Mathematical thinking is beautiful. It's simple …"

Louisa had stared at me as if I'd gone mad. "Simple!"

"Yes, simple. They explain things. They give you universal truth so you can see beauty in them."

Robbie glanced at me sideways, puzzled, unconvinced, and we went our separate ways. Cruising down Mount Pleasant Road on my bike, I remembered that conversation with Louisa and realized there was nothing except shades of grey in my life, never mind all the time I spent dealing with numbers.

∞

One Saturday afternoon after the birthday of one of my phantom siblings — Susannah this time — I was invited to Louisa's house. I couldn't wait to get away from home because more than ever it echoed with the sounds of dead babies.

The day before, Mom had made a birthday cake for Susannah, iced it elaborately with pink flowers, hung streamers from her bedroom ceiling, and in a card wrote, "Love and hugs from Mom and Dad." I'd walked quickly past her door, but even without looking, felt her tiny, ghost-like figure slither along the walls, imagined I heard an unearthly child's cry.

I'd thought Mom had really gone overboard, that what she was doing was sick, and prayed she wasn't sliding back into the crazy depression she'd had before. I was spending more and more time at Jack's — less at Robbie's after our recent conversation — but the resurrection of the tiny ghosts, and Mom's birthday cake, had reinforced my desire to get out of there.

So when Louisa invited me to spend an afternoon at her house, a mixture of anxiety and adrenaline rushed over me. I'd only been to her house once before briefly, on a weekday after school, and only Louisa's oldest brother, Kevin, had been at home. Kevin was a hulking fellow who glanced at me with curiosity, and possibly, with dismissal. Louisa and I had passed him in the kitchen when we stopped in for freshly baked muffins. She had grabbed a couple and dragged me back onto the street.

"You have no idea," she'd said as we walked together. "Our house is a pigsty. And the noise — Grand Central Station all the time. Oh, and guess who'll be hanging around making big eyes at us? My sister, Pam. I hate it. I hate *her*! She thinks she's better than everybody."

I watched Louisa's changing expressions. looked at her as she stood in the middle of the sidewalk, staring at me as though seeing me for the first time. "Ha!" she exclaimed, then laughed. "Pam might be after you, so you better watch yourself."

At that mention of Pam, my mind shifted to images of her: willowy, silent, serious, a girl at the top of her classes and admired by her teachers. *That* girl wanted my attention?

But Louisa's laugh became infectious, and I laughed, too, supposing she was into her lighthearted, teasing self. So I'd put the girl I called Shepherdess Pam out of my mind.

∞

The Blackstock home was one of those box-like houses built in the dozens in the 1930s, all of them with elongated front and back gardens. Louisa's father was trimming a hedge in the front. The garden was littered with abandoned kids' toys, an old tricycle, a broken swing set, a child's wheelbarrow. Mr. Blackstock glanced up, nodded at us, and continued his chopping.

Indoors, chaos ruled. Louisa's mom, her immense figure floating in a loose-fitting gown, spread herself over everything the way I imagined a mythical Earth Mother would do. While folding laundry in the living room, she was besieged on all sides by children of various ages, twins among them, who grabbed clothes from her and ran around, dangling them in the air, laughing, teasing, and chasing one another.

"I've got your bra, Lou!" cried one of the twin girls as she danced about, swirling it in the air.

"It's Louisa, damn you!" Louisa yelled, leaping over a two-seater couch to snatch the bra from her.

I enjoyed all this vastly. Books, toys, cushions, and all kinds of paraphernalia littered the room and covered the floor and furniture. More of the same appeared in what I could see of the dining room. I fell in love with the whole scene: the smiling mother; the teasing, laughing, boisterous children; and most of all, the relaxed, easy atmosphere. Louisa's mother, enormous, as I said, in a brightly patterned gown, nodded and smiled at me but paid me no further attention. Shepherdess Pam wasn't among the siblings, and vaguely I wondered where she was.

Louisa shared a bedroom with two of her sisters, so we went out to the back porch that, for a short time, was uninhabited by children.

"I'll get you a drink. Coffee, tea, lemonade?" she asked as we fell onto the sagging couch, Louisa making no attempt to provide the promised drinks.

"Now you see, don't you?" she muttered. "I've promised myself I'll never, like *never*, live like this. That's why I have to get out of here. My mom wouldn't even miss me. If I suddenly disappeared or if I became someone else, she wouldn't even notice, would she?"

"I'd love to live in your family," I said fervently.

Louisa pulled one of my earlobes. "You know you're a bit of a weirdo, don't you? You and Robbie and Jack. The class nerds — that's what you were called. Did you know that?"

We sat like that in idle conversation as the afternoon sun began its gentle slide, as the sounds of chaos within the house faded.

Conversation. My mind fixed itself on the word, and I remembered that Jack, like Robbie, once asked me what Louisa and I talked about.

Now, with silence stretching between us, I tried to recall

the substance of some of our previous conversations. Snippets came to me, how, apart from math, I'd tried to explain to her the colours of birdsong. That sometime I wanted her to stand outside with me in a thunderstorm to feel the fury of the natural world on her skin, in her hair, in her eyes. She'd laughed and teased me, supposing I was kidding. Once, I attempted talking about Schumann's romantic music and told her that one day I'd play some of it for her.

"Ha! Never mind that old fellow," she'd said dismissively, and changed the subject. Whatever that subject was, I couldn't remember, only that she was always laughing, teasing, and tickling me. Enveloped as I was in a haze of passion, I heard nothing except the sweet flow of her voice, saw only the shooting sparks in her eyes, and in the sunlight, a dance of the freckles on her nose.

Right now, she broke what I felt was a companionable silence between us. "Mom will expect me to properly introduce you, to get you tea or coffee." But, snuggling closer, one arm around my neck, she made no effort to move. "You don't want any, do you? Why don't we go off somewhere, get a drink — a *real* one? Besides, if we go right away, we'll miss Pammy. She'll be getting home any minute — she goes to her music lesson twice a week now."

My mind wasn't on tea, or Shepherdess Pam, but on what Louisa had said: "You know you're a bit of a weirdo, don't you?"

Yeah, how could I be anything else? I thought bitterly.

CHAPTER EIGHTEEN

That early fall I continued working with Uncle Albert; chiselled away on my carvings in the basement, mostly on a wooden raft that, theoretically, would float; and kicked around with Jack and Robbie, going to movies, playing chess, and riding our bikes down Yonge Street on Friday nights.

One weekend afternoon, using Jack's father's car with a small trailer hitched to it, we hauled my wooden raft down to Cherry Beach. Like a bunch of clowns, with much yelling and heaving and Robbie throwing in a few swear words, we got it across the sand and into the water to test its seaworthiness. Amazingly, it floated! We shouted in unison and danced around on the sand. Then, still laughing like idiots, we piled on it and tried to push one another off.

At the end of the afternoon, wet and sunburned, we dragged it back to the trailer. I felt sorry the day was over. I really liked Cherry Beach. Back then it was untamed, not manicured, not pretty, a place ignored by the hordes that swarmed other beaches.

Some weekends Jack and Robbie played tennis on the Davisville courts while I kept score in the umpire's chair. I never attempted to swing a racquet because of my lack of coordination. I would have missed most of the balls, or possibly even knocked my nose off with a racquet.

One Friday evening, Louisa and I sat on a park bench above the courts eating ice cream. "I told you my family's gone away for the weekend, didn't I?" she asked. "They're up at our cottage in Muskoka. So, dear Jules, we have the whole house to ourselves." She shot me a look that alarmed and attracted me in equal measure.

I pushed aside my fears of what I might be expected to do, thrust aside the background rumblings — earthquake proportions — on whether I should tell her about not being able to have children. If we were indeed to have a permanent relationship, to one day become engaged, then married, I needed to be honest and upfront right away. Leaning back against the park bench, I fell into a lazy, hazy cocoon of anticipation and pleasure tinged with anxiety.

When we arrived at Louisa's house, I was edgy, nervous. My eyes wandered around the room that Louisa shared with her sisters, Bonnie and Bunny. I smothered a laugh as she raced about in a hasty attempt to clean up, piling clothes in a corner and stacking papers on a small white desk.

"But it's creepy," I said. "I'm expecting one of your sisters to walk through the door any minute." In fact, for me, the empty house that echoed with the noise of parents, children, and dogs seemed creepier.

"Damn it, I've been forgetting to take the pill," Louisa said. Then, with her eyes full of mischief, she ripped off her skirt, blouse, and underclothes until she lay gloriously naked across her bed.

Blood rushed into my face. Something urgent flooded me, but I didn't … couldn't look at her. Fixing my eyes on the closed bedroom door, I stuttered, "Y-you've forgotten your … what?"

"Oh, you big innocent! The pill, you know, so I won't get pregnant."

My world spun. *"Pregnant?"* The implication that she'd done this before sank in. "But you can't get pregnant!" I wanted to shout, but the words stuck in my throat. My thoughts wrapped around and over me. I felt euphoric one moment, then cold and cheerless the next.

She's done this before. So what, you big ninny? It's what people do. The word pregnant bubbled in my mind in hot red and purple. *She said she wants children. I can't have any. If I tell her, she'll go away. But what if she pretends she doesn't care but really she does? In time she'll hold it against me. She'll come to hate me. She might even leave me for a man who can give her kids.*

My urgent, conflicted feelings rocked me. Moments passed. I moved when I heard a soft voice caressing the air. "Come on, Julian. You know what to do."

Finally, I looked down at Louisa's slim, tanned body naked before me, at her perky breasts, and for a moment thought I'd faint. How could I touch her, my idol, my pure, innocent, untouchable angel?

The voice from the bed urged, caressed, and suddenly a wild rush of ecstasy raged through me with such violence that I cried out. Then I fell upon her.

Somehow we made sweet, awkward, clumsy love, and afterward, lay happily tangled in her bedsheets.

"Never mind the pill," Louisa said as she tickled me. "A girl never gets pregnant the first time with a guy."

Through my euphoria, her words echoed: *A girl never gets pregnant the first time with a guy.* So did she just do it once with each guy if she forgot to take the pill?

In the days and weeks that followed, I staggered about, burdened by a new reality, trying to come to terms with the knowledge that what Louisa offered me wasn't new but something tried out on others before me. How many? Who with? Furthermore, she wanted kids and I couldn't give her that.

CHAPTER NINETEEN

On a late fall day, Uncle Albert died. He'd been tuning a piano in a palatial home on Moore Park's Inglewood Drive, had fallen off the stool, and died almost instantly. A major heart attack, the doctor had said.

"It was his bloody smoking did it!" Dad, who had fallen into a sort of stupor, roused himself enough to curse. "Damn filthy habit. Now it's gone and killed him!"

Mom frowned at his language, but she, too, was crushed. Tears trickled down her cheeks. She remained standing stiffly against the kitchen window, staring out blankly for so long that I worried her old, depressive state might return, or some other craziness. Now there was no Uncle Albert to help out.

No Uncle Albert! My world had suddenly become formless, bottomless, empty.

"Muriel?" Dad took Mom's hand and led her to the couch. Sinking down beside her, he put an arm clumsily around her shoulders.

"He was one of my favourite people," Mom eventually said when she stirred herself and gazed up at me. With a flash of animation that also sounded like an accusation, she added, "A positive influence on you, too, Julian." She inclined her head toward where I still slouched against the wall. "You know he raised your stature in the eyes of the world, don't you?"

In yours, you mean, I thought.

I loved Uncle Albert as much as I loved my dad. With

my uncle's unexpected dying, I truly believed some part of me had died, too. I rushed down the basement steps to the piano he'd given me and played some of his favourite Stephen Foster folk songs. Then, for him, I switched to parts of Brahms's First Symphony, caressing the keys and dampening them with my tears.

Mom yelled down the stairs that I was making too much noise, that it wasn't appropriate and I should be sitting quietly remembering Uncle Albert. "Have your dinner, too. It's getting cold."

After swallowing something that tasted vaguely like yesterday's beef stew, I ran back downstairs to play more of Uncle Albert's beloved piano pieces. But this time the yellowed and chipped keys, like stained teeth, grinned horribly at me, and I shrank from them. The tiled walls and floor closed in on me, and for a long time I couldn't touch the piano. Instead, I played my recording of the Beatles hit "Uncle Albert/Admiral Halsey." Above me I heard footsteps, voices, the clamour of those calling to offer condolences, so I remained with my arms wrapped around myself in the basement, hiding in Uncle Albert's world, the one he'd introduced me to, a place of beautiful sounds and instruments, of other, different voices, and most of all, of uncritical love.

∞

A few days later, in our lawyer's office, I sat close to Mom and held her hand as we learned that Uncle Albert had left my parents his investments.

"Oh, oh, no!" she exclaimed, then wept, rocking her body wildly back and forth in her chair.

Dad looked at her with alarm, held her other hand, and made placating noises.

"To you, Julian, his nephew," our lawyer intoned, "your

Uncle Albert leaves you his apartment on St. Clair Avenue." The lawyer was a youngish fellow with a long, thin face topped with light brown hair closely cut around his ears. "He also leaves you his baby grand Steinway piano and all his other musical instruments. As well, he leaves you his car." The young man placed the file on his desk and removed his glasses. "A nice piece of property for a youngster, I'd say. Now to his brother, Robert, he leaves the money in his savings account."

Dad muttered something under his breath, but Mom maintained everything was as it should be, since Uncle Robert was Uncle Albert's brother, too. When the amount was read out, I realized it actually wasn't that much.

I stared at Mom and Dad, my mouth hanging open, questions on my tongue, but neither of them seemed surprised.

"Why Uncle Robert?" I asked. "I mean, we hardly ever see him. And we never even talk about him, like he's someone unmentionable, maybe even a criminal." But I didn't say that last part aloud.

I'd only seen Uncle Robert two or three times since I'd finished high school, and there was only one photo of him in our house and none in Uncle Albert's. He wasn't much like Dad or Uncle Albert to look at, either: paunchy, dark hair cut short, sides and back, unsmiling. That one and only photo must have been taken when he was in his twenties. In the past year or two, I'd heard veiled comments through Dad's one-sided telephone conversations with Uncle Albert: Uncle Robert giving up his print shops, travelling around the Middle East, something about weapons, drugs — or maybe I'd imagined that part because of all the secrecy. I also wondered what had happened to Steve. Where was he?

I pushed such thoughts aside as exhilaration mixed with inexpressible sorrow settled over me. Then came a nagging feeling about Steve not getting anything. I conjured him up:

a bulky fellow close to me in age, always in oversized sweats or T-shirts, jeans that hung below his hips. In his voice, I saw faded colours, sometimes laced with bolts of black. The times when Dad needed his assistance, when Uncle Albert asked if he could help him move his piano — he would pay him — Steve never showed up, was never there, never available. Other images floated in my mind: the peculiar-shaped head crunched on thick shoulders, a neck that thrust forward, eyes that changed hue from brackish brown to weedy green. When I thought of him at all, unaccountable pity for him because of how we'd been as boys alternated with dislike. Pity because he hadn't had a father like mine. But he also hadn't had a mother like mine!

When we left the lawyer's office, my head still spinning with the news that I'd inherited an apartment, I leaned forward in the car and asked, "Really, Mom and Dad, what's going on? Why did Uncle Albert leave all of that to me and nothing at all to Steve?"

"I can't speak for your uncle about Steve," Dad said. "I don't really know anything. But as for you, your Uncle Albert thought of you as his son —"

He stopped, and into a thickening silence, Mom added, "He never had children of his own, as you know."

I knew that Aunt Clarissa had died a year after Uncle Albert married her, that he'd never connected with another woman. No one had ever told me what my aunt had died of, and back then I hadn't asked. Now, for the first time, I did.

"She had an infection," Mom said.

"What sort of infection?"

"It's one you get in childbirth," Dad said. "She died, and the baby, too."

Dad looked as if he was going to say something else, but Mom raised a hand to her lips and said we'd talk about it another time.

I felt confused and shut out of something that involved me. At home I walked up the driveway into our house, and despite my inheritance, felt stripped naked, emptied of all emotions. Upstairs in my room, I lay on my bed and stared at the ceiling.

Uncle Albert dead.

Suddenly flush with money I didn't feel was mine.

Louisa thinking she couldn't get pregnant. Louisa having sex with other guys.

I recalled what Uncle Albert had said about Mom when her babies died, and now part of me wanted to die, too. I didn't really mean it, of course, and the feeling didn't last, but I knew I'd never forget my uncle. He was the most important person in my life, and I'd lost something huge and irreplaceable. A pain in my heart became so intense I felt as though it might crack.

CHAPTER TWENTY

Over time, my thoughts returned to Louisa, unhappy ones tangled with fleeting moments of excitement. As in a bad dream that didn't end at daybreak, I fought with myself: I loved her, but how much did I really know about her? If I told her I couldn't have kids, she'd pretend she didn't want them. But, as Mom had said, she might come to regret that later on and then hate me.

I paced absent-mindedly, sat staring at the walls in my bedroom, ate my dinner in silence, until Mom finally said, "Wake up, Julian. Wake up!"

She figured I was still crying for Uncle Albert, and it annoyed her. *It's not a competition about who's grieving the most!* I wanted to yell. *As though my grief is somehow disloyal to you and Dad.* But there was no way I could explain the depth of my uncle's loss. Nor could I ask her whether I should tell Louisa I couldn't have babies. It was just one more layer of misery.

Dull, featureless days passed until one morning I awoke to early-morning sunlight filtering through my bedroom window. I thrust aside the curtains and saw not sunbeams across the lawn but black shadows, no colours anywhere. Flopping back onto my bed, I stared at the ceiling and willed Uncle Albert to come and tell me what I should do. Then, in vague, formless silhouette, he did. His brow wrinkled in concentration and his lips moved, but no words came out.

He kept shaking his head, then slowly the silhouette — or whatever I was seeing — faded, and something rigid and cold hardened inside me. I got up and went out without breakfast into the sunlight. But the house, the garden, the streets, everything, lay in shadows. I glanced up at the trees, but the birds were silent. Aimlessly, I walked up and down Mount Pleasant Road, up and down and up again, coiled tightly inside myself. A blackbird screeched in front of me, noisy and quarrelsome. I looked at it, then knew what I had to do.

For weeks I prepared, trying out the words: *I can't do it. I won't. I must. I can't.* Late that evening, I phoned and asked Louisa to meet me at the corner of Mount Pleasant and Belsize the next day at 4:00 p.m., then slept little or not at all that night.

In the afternoon as I walked to Belsize for our meeting, thunderclouds threatened a downpour. As soon as I met Louisa at the corner, we strode across Yonge Street and into the cemetery from that entrance. I could tell she knew something momentous was about to happen. Still with few words between us, we threaded our way through the headstones. The sky continued to darken in the west, clouds looming like smeared charcoal. Rain seemed imminent. I decided to get what I had to say over with so we could get home before the deluge. About to destroy my life, I was worried about getting wet!

Before I opened my mouth to begin, Louisa asked, "You want to make love in the rain among the headstones?" Laughing, she grabbed my hands. "Up here, come on." Then she climbed atop a wide, blackened headstone.

"Desecration," I replied, but climbed up beside her. Sheltered beneath the hanging branches of an old willow tree, we sat side by side, the dying blooms of a nearby rose of Sharon bush reaching out almost to touch us.

"If I didn't know better, I'd think you've been avoiding

me," she said, peering into my eyes with a severe expression. In a gesture familiar to me, she flicked a strand of her hair that had grown long in the past few months, then touched my cheeks, my eyebrows, my lips, and leaned close to kiss me. Still laughing, she flipped up her skirt. "Really, Jules, where on earth have you been hiding?"

"I told you about Uncle Albert. I can't believe he's dead. I miss him dreadfully." What I didn't say was that I would have given anything to talk to him right now.

Pressure built in my chest, and damning everything to hell, I jumped off the headstone and squeezed my knuckles together savagely. *I am going to tell her.* I stood stiffly, arms across my chest, gazing up at her, unblinking. I felt like somebody else, not like me at all. With my heart thudding hard against my ribs, I reached up, gripped her arm roughly, and pulled her off the headstone. Then I put my palms on her cheeks and forced her to look at me. "Listen, Lou, I've got something to say —"

"Louisa," she interrupted automatically, staring back at me, curious, not yet clueing into my mood.

I glanced down at the overgrown grass around the headstone, the few faded flowers wilting at its base. Summoning all the little things I'd silently criticized her for, I forced myself to remember how she'd flirted with and teased all the guys, drew them on, then dropped them. How many fellows had she made love to before me? God only knew! I stared hard at her, gathering my resentments, interpreting all her behaviour in light of what I considered my new insights. I worked myself up to hate her, but at the same time loathing with every bone in my body what I was about to say.

Aware of my silence, of the hard expression on my face as I looked at her, but still not really picking up on my mood, or not believing it, she tilted her chin at me, flicked her hair over a shoulder with that old, seductive gesture. When I remained quiet, she cocked her head to one side and batted heavily pencilled eyes at me.

That was it! Suddenly, I hated those gestures, hated the way she flicked her hair, jiggled her body, tilted her head. How her painted eyelashes fluttered on cheeks rosy with blush. I saw myself, too: big ears, square jaw, large forehead, all the clumsy six feet of me. I saw my mother's frosty eyes on me filled with disappointment; Dad, except for rare moments, falling into line behind her; Uncle Albert, eyes permanently closed. Now I loathed myself, too.

"Jules, you're scaring me! Why are you looking at me like that? It's like you … you hate me …"

"I do hate you!" I burst out, and at that moment, relieved at the opening she'd offered, believed it. "I never loved you. Never! I pretended, just to see if I could get you. I don't want you anymore … you should just go, go away from me and flutter your eyes at one of those poor suckers who drool all over you. Go have all their babies, since that's what you want."

"Babies?" She seemed astonished. "*I* want babies?"

I didn't see her expression of incredulity, how her eyes had widened in shock, because I'd turned my back on her. Whatever else she said was drowned out by a loud clap of thunder, and in the next minute, fat raindrops fell.

"I mean it!" I moved a few feet to the shelter of the willow tree. "I'm going away, and you're not to look for me. If you try, I swear you'll never find me." My body shook all over, my lips quivered. A tight feeling in my chest became a sharp pain, and my blood felt hot and thick in my veins. I had an urgent need to sit, but the grass was wet.

A quick glance showed me Louisa's eyes had widened further into black pools, her face blotched a furious red. She jerked her head, and fervently I hoped reality had finally gripped her. I hoped — God only knew what I hoped.

"Well, I think you've gone mad," she said, reaching

forward and grabbing the lapels of my jacket. She stared up at me, an uncertain smile on her face that only faded when she fully registered my expression.

Weirdly, a sudden laugh escaped me. "I just wanted to see if I could get you." I laughed again. "I never did love you. Anyway, you don't have to worry. You've never had any problems getting guys to fall all over you. Guys are so stupid!" I stood there with my arms folded, continuing to marshal my anger, the sense of betrayal I felt about all the boys I supposed she'd made out with before me — maybe after me, as well. At that moment I chose to believe she had in order to feed my rage.

I turned to walk away, but my feet wouldn't move. Risking another quick glance at her, I saw a collision of feelings twisting her face, watched as it turned into hard, chiselled stone. And then she was gone like all the little ghosts in the phantom babies' bedrooms at home.

Feeling sick, dizzy, as if the world were spinning off its axis and I would surely topple off, I tried to move, get myself home ... but my feet refused to obey me. Sometime later I did budge, stumbled over a tree root, and fell headlong among long grass and mounds of leaves. I had no recollection how long I lay on the wet ground, or how long rain drenched me through the branches of the willow tree. After pulling myself up, I slouched home along wet pavement, only vaguely aware the world had become silent: no bird sounds, no wind in the grass, no traffic noise on the streets, until thunder again clapped overhead and rain once more whipped at me in sheets — somehow a fitting atmosphere for the end of a fairy-tale dream.

I walked and kept walking. Wet streets, the darkened walls of buildings, and the imposing structure of the school itself closed in around me amid the crash of the elements. Ghouls stalked me, maybe the ghosts of all my phantom siblings. Someone else, too. On the slippery pavement a familiar figure zigzagged ahead of me. I thought for a minute that it was Steve because of the crush of his head on his shoulders, the way he swung his arms as he strode forward. It seemed these days that I sighted him everywhere. Had he, too, become a phantom, as I'd thought once before?

∞

"I told her," I said to Mom. I'd come into the kitchen soaking wet and stood dripping water over the floor. Mom lifted her hands from a pastry board. "Don't walk in here with all your wet stuff on! Get your shoes off!"

Still, I stood there, vaguely taking in Mom's domestic scene: the little transistor radio in the corner by the toaster playing pop songs from the 1940s, a romance novel open beside the pastry bowl, a row of cupcakes already frosted.

"Cakes for one of your missing children?" I asked. "Oh, yes, Jeremy's birthday, or is it Susannah's?" I heard the bitterness in my voice. "Happy birthday, you stupid dead kid! Mom, here's something that'll make you happy — Louisa's gone. Gone forever. Go tell that to all your missing children you're always talking to. Go on!"

In the months that followed, I slid into what I called my Dark Age, cut off from sights, sounds, and colours. I felt cold, felt my nerves sharp, ragged, my breath shuddering when I talked, which wasn't much. While I did carry on Uncle Albert's business tuning pianos, I no longer saw the colours of the different keys. I suppose I must have done an okay job, since I was asked to return, and in time became familiar with the insides of swanky homes in Rosedale and Forest Hill, in Lawrence Park and York Mills, and also in apartments downtown. I didn't have to push off sexy middle-aged housewives, since my blank, or better still, my black expression, told them not even to try.

CHAPTER TWENTY-ONE

Uncle Albert had once introduced me to his boss, Ted Bilson, at the Clarkson Gordon accounting office on Bay Street where my father had also worked but at a different location. Mr. Bilson had given me odd jobs to do. Sometimes he'd drop in, and I'd found myself liking him immediately — his quiet manner, the warmth in his eyes.

When Uncle Albert showed Mr. Bilson some of the work I'd done for him, Mr. Bilson whistled and told me I had a job there any time just for the asking. Now I needed one, needed the money, and to work there would be like holding on to whatever I could of Uncle Albert. So I went to Clarkson Gordon and asked for Mr. Bilson.

"Sir, I'd very much like to work here, to work for you," I said when I was ushered into his office, looking him straight in the eye. "Not to try to replace my uncle, of course," I added hastily. "If you have anything for me, I'll be grateful. I'm afraid I don't have much proper training or qualifications, but I'm willing to do anything, to learn everything. Actually, I don't know very much ..."

"I know what you can do," Mr. Bilson replied, and hired me on the spot, at first for a part-time position.

When I arrived on my first day, he put me in Uncle Albert's old office. On the walls stood his collection of books, on his desk a pile of folders, his computer, a pen holder. The very air smelled of him, something still and warm and musky. I pictured him in his tweed jacket over a crisp white shirt, bending over his papers, chin in one hand, forehead crinkled in concentration. A faint image of him arose right there in front of me, and I felt dizzy. Holding the door frame for support, I turned my back to Mr. Bilson to wipe away my tears.

∞

Years passed, but I was hardly aware of their passage as I focused on my job at Clarkson Gordon and dealt with my angst over what had happened with Louisa. One day a new request came for me to look at a piano on Lawrence Park Crescent. Just another rich, bored housewife to fend off, I supposed, and even though it was a flowery spring day, I was in one of my black moods. Even walking past two miniature lions guarding a wrought-iron gate, past a spreading lilac bush forming a canopy over the patio, didn't alter it. I knocked and waited, staring at my feet. I cracked my knuckles, preparing myself to dislike this rich housewife even before I saw her.

The door finally opened, and there stood a young woman, vastly different from others I'd dealt with in similar wealthy houses.

"Yes?" she asked, her voice and manner abrupt.

"I'm the piano tuner."

"Oh. Good, you're on time. I heard about your Uncle Albert. I'm sorry."

"Yes." I contemplated my feet again.

"Follow me." Her voice had resumed a peremptory tone.

I walked after her tall, reed-like figure as she moved with short, quick steps on the hardwood floors into what she called the drawing room. I guessed her age to be close to thirty, but it was hard to tell for sure.

"There," she said.

I shifted my eyes from her to glimpse a baby grand Yamaha piano in the middle of the vast room. Above it hung a print of Renoir's *Young Girls at the Piano*.

"I'm not sure what's wrong. I had it tuned just three weeks ago by someone who's been servicing it off and on for years, but the sound isn't quite right. I thought I'd get a second opinion. I'll play something and you can tell me what you think." She sat on the piano stool and ran her fingers over the keys, then launched into something unfamiliar to me. When she stopped, I asked who the composer was.

"Stravinsky, an excerpt from his *Rite of Spring*. Do you know it?"

"No."

"What do you think of it?"

"It's, well, a bit …"

"Revolutionary. Some call it destructive modernist. Others say it's all unresolved dissonances. I like it. Let me play you something else." She shot me a cool, direct look before turning back to the piano.

Immediately, I recognized Schumann's *Sonatas for the Young*. As her fingers danced over the keys, the large room filled with soft spangles of colour. I remained with my gaze on the woman whose fingers produced the sounds. Her form was sharp, angular, descending in a long line that had no shape. The profile turned to me revealed a finely chiselled chin, a long, thin nose, a neckline hidden by a buttoned-up blouse tucked into a straight skirt that fell almost to her narrow feet encased in flat-bottomed sandals.

When she finished, her fingers lingered over the keys for a moment. She stood up then and crossed the room, her movements calm and deliberate. Within a few feet of me, she looked directly into my eyes. Strange to recount, but an immediate sense of relief fell over me. In those few seconds, I felt I was in the presence of someone clear, uncomplicated, and immediately decipherable, someone with no hidden agenda. More than that, an air of solidity, a kind of imperturbability, surrounded her. I was filled with a sense of comfort, and again, of relief. All of this in the first few moments.

"Well, what do you think?" she asked.

"I can check the piano again for you, but it sounds fine to me." I opened my bag, took out my tuning fork, and tuned it to A, then the octave A above and below it. I sounded this interval as the two notes together, listening for a beat in the sound, then moved on to other notes in that scale. "It's fine. Do you want to play something else and I'll listen again?" Even though she had said little, had sat without moving in a straight-backed chair, I felt myself smiling at the quiet air about her.

She returned the smile. "Would you like to stay and have coffee with me?"

"Thank you, but I've got another appointment. If you want, I could come back, say, in two weeks, to check your piano."

"Yes, please do, if you can spare the time."

I'll move the earth to make the time, I thought as I left her and swung down the path between the spouting lions.

Two weeks later, as we sat over cups of coffee in her parents' palatial home, I felt myself enveloped in a warm kind of harmony, wrapped in a blanket of contentment. All the tension in my arms, shoulders, and neck fell away. The dominant colour I came to see in Penny was the sound of F sharp major.

When I was alone again, I said to myself, "This must be love." I laughed and punched the air. "Love — this is it!"

Eventually, timidly, I asked her out on a date, and matter-of-factly, she accepted. I brought her flowers, plucked one, and was about to tuck it behind her ear when she stopped me and handed it back. Smiling, she said, "Julian, that's not me."

A special education teacher, she played the piano for all school concerts. "How fortuitous that you can be on hand to keep it tuned," she told me. But she smiled as she said it, and I thought again that this must be what love feels like. To me her sharp features, the long, thin form of her, were beautiful. The woman I'd first seen on a piano stool creating beautiful music, the woman remote and self-contained, became the woman holding hands with me in her tranquil garden.

CHAPTER TWENTY-TWO

My subsequent dates with Penny reinforced my sense that she was my destiny. Her parents liked me, even though they didn't know about my inheritance and must have supposed I didn't have much of an income. Obviously, it wasn't important to them. But there was the thing about having kids.

"Penny doesn't want children," I said when I first talked about her to Mom and Dad. It took me a long time to do this.

"Don't believe her." My mother's hands, full of a lavender cloth with yellow patterns on it, didn't pause. I noticed a *Women's World* magazine open on the counter. "All women want them."

Mom was wrong.

"You've got to tell her," Mom kept telling me after each of Penny's visits.

It was during one of these times that Penny asked if she could see the house. "It's larger than most on this street, a bit unusual, and semi-detached," she commented.

"It's more ridiculously unusual than you'll ever guess," I said, but so softly she didn't hear me.

"Oh, not today," Mom said quickly. "I'm doing a big cleanup, and I'm afraid it's a bit of a mess upstairs."

"Maybe another time," Penny said, obviously disappointed. Then suddenly she cocked her head. "There seems to be an old nursery song playing from somewhere up there."

She pointed at the stairs. "Julian, can you hear it? Am I hearing things?"

"No," I lied. "I don't hear anything."

It was only after Penny saw the baby seat in the back of our Buick that Mom had left parked in front of the house, after she asked me what was going on, that I told her the truth.

Penny listened without interrupting me, her expression thoughtful. "Postpartum depression," she eventually said. "My guess is that she wasn't treated and her only way of coping was to create and hold on to this morbid fantasy. How very sad for her. And for your dad. But most of all, for you, Julian. However —" and here she became brisk "— you have to accept it and get on with things, which obviously you've done."

And that was it. She made no further reference to it until many years later.

One warm spring day I took Penny to Mount Pleasant Cemetery. She knew I walked there often to listen to birdsong and other sounds of the earth, but this time I knew she expected something else. Among the richness of flowering forsythia and bluebells, I said, "Penny, there's something I have to tell you."

At the tone of my voice, the light in her eyes disappeared instantly, replaced by a look of alarm.

"Look, I can't have kids," I said, not looking at her. "I had mumps when I was sixteen and became sterile. I'm so sorry if I let you believe —"

"Julian, stop. You didn't lead me to believe anything." She hesitated, then asked, "Do you love me?" Her face was flushed, head held at a sharp angle as she gazed up at me.

"Good God, yes!"

"So never mind about kids. I have enough of them all day at school. Besides, I'm getting a bit old to have them."

She hesitated again, then added, "On that subject, I probably can't get pregnant, anyway, because of a condition I had called endometriosis. It affects the lining of the uterus ... well, never mind all the details, you and I, we won't worry about having kids. We can be happy without them."

I wouldn't say I was happy at the idea we'd be without kids, because deep down, of course, I wanted them, well, at least one, but I'd lived long enough with the knowledge I was sterile that her bald statement hardly affected me.

Right then I said, "Hey, you're not much older than I am."

She didn't say it, and I didn't think it until later, that it was probably a good thing I couldn't have children because of my ill-fated genes.

We embraced each other with relief and gratitude, agreeing that we didn't need kids, anyway. I proposed to her, and we strolled out of Mount Pleasant Cemetery hand in hand to a flower shop where I bought the largest bunch of blood-red roses I could carry. Then we headed for my parents' house.

When we got there, I said, almost breathlessly, "Mom, Dad, Penny and I are getting married."

Mom was seated in the living room, her lap covered in the same lavender-and-yellow cloth she'd been stitching earlier. FM radio played old love songs of the 1950s. She glanced up at us and gave one of her rare smiles.

Mom did approve of Penny and of our marrying. "But not yet," she told us. "Julian's still young." She didn't need to say that Penny wasn't. "He needs to establish himself further at Clarkson Gordon."

After Penny was gone, as usual, Mom warned, "She'll want children no matter what she says now. All women do." Her voice was flat, her eyes dull. "She might say she doesn't want them now, but she'll hold it against you later, and then what?"

Soon after our announcement, I contacted the company managing Uncle Albert's affairs and said I intended to take possession of his apartment. After it was vacated, bit by bit, I moved into it. I took only my clothes, books, the musical instruments I'd been working on, and my transistor radio and alarm clock, leaving my uncle's piano where it was. Uncle Albert's place, rented out since his death, had everything else. That first night, full of bittersweet memories, I slept in his bed. In the morning, my pillow was damp with tears.

I waited until Mom had gone out before I moved a few other things, worried that any change in routine — it could be any little thing — might set her off into depression again, or whatever her condition was called. The two of us had always had a difficult relationship, but I was her only living son. I was moving out of the house, and it was all a big change for her. Now my phantom siblings could have the whole house to themselves, I thought, and Mom could have unlimited time to spend with them.

Mom's emotions were twisted, I could see. At moments when she looked straight at me, she didn't seem to see me. Sometimes she walked as though in a trance, and I fretted further about her. But I also couldn't wait to get out of that house.

∞

"I'm a no-fuss person," Penny told me. "Are you happy with a small, low-key wedding? I'm not one for the big white dress and bridesmaids tripping after me."

"No long white train? No crown on your beautiful head? And no troop of little flower girls at your pretty feet?" I smiled at the incongruity of the images.

"Quick, simple, no fuss — that's me."

The sharp lines on Penny's face softened as she smiled and

leaned forward to drop a kiss on my forehead. I put aside my momentary disappointment, telling myself I certainly didn't need a big splash. I felt ridiculously happy and punched the air.

Later, after Penny and I were married, Mom showed how pleased she was by offering to do whatever she could to help Penny settle into Uncle Albert's apartment. "I'll make you your first dinner when you move in, Penny."

"Maybe you can take your Uncle Albert's piano now," Dad suggested.

"Well, I would, but there won't be room for two, what with Penny's piano." I smiled. "On the other hand, there would be one for each of us."

"You can leave it where it is for now, of course," Dad said, "until you get a bigger place and can take it."

∞

Soon after our small wedding and Penny and I were settled in Uncle Albert's apartment, I said, "Penny, I never want to leave here. It's full of my uncle, his warmth, the colours of his music, his books." I didn't say it, but I also felt comfortable inside myself in a way I never had. I was married to a wonderful, sensible woman. I had a job in the place where Uncle Albert had worked, and I lived in his old home.

From time to time, we invited Mom and Dad to visit, quite often at first, sometimes together with Penny's parents. Those events were a bit strained, but overall I thought Mom seemed reasonably well. I never asked her what she did with my old bedroom, but did wonder if she moved Jeremy out of his makeshift room in the hallway and put him in it. And I never did know the fate of my dead, my unborn, and stillborn siblings, because I never went upstairs in that house again.

One thing I did do, though, was to begin avoiding Mount Pleasant Road, in fact, all of North Toronto. A weird sense had crept up on me that the scenes surrounding my old relationship with Louisa might contaminate my new one with Penny. Those times I visited Mom and Dad I rode my bike, sometimes drove Uncle Albert's car south to Moore Avenue, across it and up Bayview, and so approached Merton Street from its east end.

"Why, Julian?" Penny would ask. "What are you dodging?"

Worried she might think less of me, I'd never mentioned Louisa to her, so, of course, I couldn't tell Penny I was afraid I might accidentally see my old flame and didn't want to frequent any of the places we'd been together. I might have been good at quashing my emotions or at shuffling them off into some inaccessible part of me, but I still didn't want to risk stirring up old memories. I even went as far as insisting on meeting Jack or Robbie somewhere downtown, on Yonge Street, at Cherry Beach, anywhere but Mount Pleasant Road.

Only one thing blotted those days of perfect happiness — the sense that someone was still following me, a shadowy shape behind me on the sidewalks around Yonge and St. Clair, a hooded figure sliding out of our building's elevator as I entered or left it. My thoughts flitted to Louisa's family, to her brother, Kevin. Had Louisa told him what I'd done to her and was he looking to exact revenge on her behalf? I remembered his expression as he'd stared at me in the kitchen of the Blackstock home, recalled his hulking figure. I wouldn't want to tangle with him.

But he wasn't the one stalking me.

One evening I lounged in a chair by the window overlooking St. Clair. Bach's Christmas Oratorio was playing at high volume — it had to compete with the noise of streetcars rattling below the window. I had a gin and tonic waiting for Penny, and a tray of cheese from a shop on Church Street. At a pause in the music I heard the front doorknob rattling. I knew it couldn't be Penny, not yet. I got up, opened the door, and caught sight of a hooded figure jiggling the lock.

"What the hell!" I shouted, raising my fists. "What do you think you're doing?"

The figure straightened, the hood fell away from his face, and an emaciated Steve in the doorway took a step back. Dressed in loose black jeans and black shirt, tattoos down his right arm, he fixed his stone-coloured eyes on me, his first expression of alarm immediately replaced by a flare of old anger.

My arms dropped to my sides, my shock at the sight of him morphing into a mix of astonishment and pity.

"Yo, cousin Julian, you're now the ripe old landowner." As he spoke, bruised colours sharpened in the hallway air. Casual now, he slouched against the door frame, hands in his pockets. "Uncle Albert's princeling boy genius." Bitterness was in his voice. "You got it all. Me? Nothing — zero. Zippo. I figure you owe me, you know, share your fortune or else …"

"Wait!" I cried in astonishment, even as a knot of guilt grew in me. "I hardly got a fortune!"

"I can contest Uncle Albert's will in court." The words sounded rehearsed.

My jaw fell, and I raised my eyes. "You … you won't get far when I say how you tried to steal from me just now."

"Not steal, since you don't keep your dough in here — or do you? I just came to see what nice things you've got."

Share my fortune? My irritation rose. Why now? Where had he been all this time? Why behave *this* way? Still with my hand on the doorknob, blocking his view of our hall, I demanded, "So what else will you do besides sue me?"

"I'll tell your precious Penny what you did to Louisa. Bet you never told her." His lips curled in a sneer. "I bet she won't admire you for that." Steve's voice had become a drawl, his expression a leer. Drawing a cigarette from his pocket, he fumbled in his pocket for a lighter.

"You can't smoke in here," I said.

"Do I care?" He inhaled and blew smoke in my face. "This is what you'll do. Sell this place and give me half. You've got a job. Your wife earns good money. So, to my way of thinking, you've got lots of dough to spare. Half should be mine, anyway."

My mouth was still hanging open when the elevator clanged and footsteps clicked on the hallway floor. It might be Penny! Panic rose in me. My voice hoarse with urgency, I whispered, "Let me think about it. Give me time. I'll contact you."

"I know where you live. I know where your wife works." With these words flung over his shoulder, Steve was gone like a spook from the underworld.

I put away this encounter in a compartment in my mind, telling myself I'd examine what to do about it some other time. Part of me couldn't imagine Steve following through on his threats, certainly not the lawsuit part. Part of me also truly felt I really did owe him.

Right now, and not only because of Steve's threats, I thought there was something else Penny and I should do: move away from this area of the city, away from all the memories, all those bits of shrapnel that could jump up from the past and hit me without warning. Penny, who had just received an award for best teacher of the year, was thinking about changing schools.

"I've been here much too long," she said of the Davisville School where she'd been teaching for a number of years. "I need more challenges or different ones. It was a good school, good kids, and a nice area of the city, but dear Julian, it's time to move on."

When the time came, to the surprise of both of us, we

relocated to Vancouver. Penny received an offer from a school on West Georgia Street downtown. Immediately, I applied for positions in accounting offices there, and it didn't take long for me, too, to receive an invitation from a prestigious firm on West Georgia Street, partly, maybe mostly, because of Mr. Bilson's recommendation.

CHAPTER TWENTY-THREE

"Penny, guess what? Mom and Dad are selling their house." I'd come home from work early that afternoon, and hearing footsteps clicking along the corridor, stood in the doorway with a glass of white wine for her. We'd been established in our Coal Harbour condo for only six months, having commuted from Port Moody all the years we'd been on the West Coast to save up for it. Mom and Dad had already flown over to see it. "They want to buy a condo," I said as Penny shrugged out of her spring jacket and kicked off her high-heeled shoes. "They were impressed with ours and want to get something like it. What do you think?"

"Well!" Penny took a sip from her glass and dropped into an armchair by the living room window. Doubt clouded her eyes. "What do you think your mom's going to do about her phantom babies' bedrooms?" She half drained her glass, picked up her school bag, turned, and emptied its contents onto the kitchen table.

"Beats me," I said. "I'll have to fly over and help them. I'll only be two or three days."

∞

Toronto in late August glinted in colours warm and honey-like. I stood with Dad in the front garden of my childhood home, late-summer phlox nodding over the path, petunias to perfume it. The sun was warm on our backs.

"Thirty-nine years, Dad," I said. "That's how long you and Mom have lived here." I hesitated, then cleared my throat. "What ... what will Mom do without the babies? Will she try to find a place for them in the condo?"

Mom, out of earshot, was bending over the dying blooms of hostas under the windowsills, smiling, frowning.

"She'll give them up. She'll have to." We stared away from each other and nothing further was said.

Their new condo was on Merton Street west of Mount Pleasant Road — the same street backing onto the same cemetery. Its little balcony on the second floor overlooked the graveyard, but the view was right into some tall maples. *Beautiful*, I thought, *because you can't see any headstones.* I'd hoped they would move away from the cemetery altogether, but that was okay.

The condo was a lot smaller than their old house, which meant a lot of downsizing. The big thing for Mom, of course, was what she would do with her missing children, their beds, furniture, toys. Nothing was mentioned among the three of us. As it happened, I wouldn't be here when the movers came because I'd been summoned to our firm's Toronto office to work on an urgent problem.

"I'm sorry, Dad," I said. "I'll be quick, but if you have to pay extra moving costs, I'll pay them." Again neither Dad nor I could mention the babies' bedrooms. Their cots weren't unloaded off the moving truck, and the spare bedroom in the new condo remained eerily bare.

Later, Penny asked me on the phone what Mom had done about the phantom babies.

"I really don't know. I can't tell yet."

"She'll adjust. She'll find a substitution. People do. I mean, you can't just get rid of an addiction, an obsession, hallucination, or whatever you want to call it, without replacing it with something else."

"I suppose, no, of course not." In my mind, I hoped whatever that something became, it would be benign.

∞

Not long after my parents were installed in their new condo, I asked Mom about Steve.

"Steve?" Mom seemed surprised, even bewildered. "Why are you asking about him now?" Suspicion entered her voice. "Who's been talking about him?"

"Nobody. If you want to know, I've always been curious for exactly that reason. No one ever talks about him. It's as if he doesn't exist." I chose not to mention his attempted break-in at our Toronto apartment before we moved to Vancouver.

"In a way, for his family, he doesn't," Dad said in his usual quiet voice. In jeans and a light blue buttoned-up shirt, he stood at the glass doors to the balcony overlooking the trees in the cemetery, a copy of *Maclean's* magazine dangling in one hand. He turned back to me. "Look, it won't hurt you to know. Steve has had an unfortunate life. I think you always understood that. As a teenager, he got into drugs …

"Drugs!"

"There was a time he got himself together and worked up north — at Camp Wood, I believe. He was in charge of rope and rock climbing. After that, well, at some point he found out your Uncle Albert had left him out of his will and you got the apartment. He was pretty mad at you, thought you'd sucked up to get the inheritance. Once, I think he tried to find you and made noises about suing you to get his share."

The light went out of Dad's eyes. Mom, in the kitchen, rattled dishes in the sink.

"Well, it wasn't really fair," I said. "He should've got something. Where is he now?"

"We haven't told him you're in Vancouver. But, son, you don't owe him anything."

Dad was about to add something further when Mom interrupted. "Steve's crazy," she said flatly. "He's been in and out of rehab institutions all these years, but even his parents don't know where he is right now."

So craziness runs right through our family, I thought. *A good thing, after all, that I can't have kids.*

CHAPTER TWENTY-FOUR

"Julian!"

"What ... what is it?" Alarm filled me at the rebuke in Penny's voice. I opened my eyes and glanced about to see several pairs of eyes fixed on me, all filled with curiosity and concern. I must have fallen asleep, and in the middle of dinner company, too.

After my return from Toronto, I was preoccupied by thoughts about Steve while still trying to rid my mind of Louisa, to push her into a mental compartment and shut the door. I hadn't thought that being back in Toronto would awaken memories of her, but it did. To banish them, I invoked images of my courtship of Penny, summoning that beautifully serene time when I was about to propose marriage to her. Filled with the joy of that time, I looked up and smiled warmly at Penny, at the two couples leaning forward in their chairs the way people do when they feel tense, or particularly involved in an unfolding drama.

"So very sorry," I said to them all. "I was remembering the time when I met Penny, and I guess I just got lost in it."

"Well, do tell us," my colleague, Jill, from our accounting office said.

Seeking to soften the hard lines on Penny's face, I launched into the story about how I worked with my Uncle Albert tuning pianos, and that was how I'd met her.

"In a home near Lawrence and Bayview, a beautiful girl

called Penny sat at a piano," I said, smiling across at my wife. "First, she played a piece by Stravinsky, then a romantic Schumann sonata. She looked untouchable like a … like a queen, so remote, so elegant. I remember she wore a long skirt and had a high-necked blouse tucked into it. She was … she was …" Overcome with the feeling that always flooded over me when I recalled that image, I couldn't finish the thought. "She stopped playing," I finally continued. "She got up from the piano stool and walked toward me."

Of course, I didn't say it, but after my heartache over Louisa, I remembered how I'd decided in that moment that Penny must be my destiny.

"Oh!" Penny looked confused, but slowly the hard lines of her face softened.

That evening, after the guests were gone, after I cleaned up the mess of dishes everywhere — I couldn't even remember what we'd had for dinner — I sat in the large armchair overlooking Coal Harbour and allowed my mind to return to that good and peaceful time in my life.

∞

A year passed, then more years. Vague restlessness began to plague me. Mentally, I surveyed my nice, good, predictable life, but as I'd discovered about some of my male co-workers, I felt the need for a jolt of something, a new project, a new challenge. As well, the sensation of having travelled far and long with something unresolved still nagged at me, the same notion I'd entertained since the fateful thirtieth-anniversary party we'd hosted earlier this year.

One Saturday, after a night of poor sleep, I got up, pulled on a dressing gown I hadn't worn in months, and stumbled into the kitchen to brew strong coffee. Something sharp poked through the dressing gown pocket as I reached for the pot. A photograph fragment. I gaped at Louisa's face staring out at me. "Holy heaven and hell!" Rudely jolted right out of my mind, of my body, I fell into an armchair and covered my eyes, the photo still crunched in my palm. But Louisa's laughing face remained sharply etched, beckoning me. Memories, like dust motes in the air, floated over and around me, bittersweet, shocking, disturbing. An inky image, sharp, claw-like, appeared behind my eyes, and I scrubbed at them with my knuckles.

Making a snap decision, I held the photo up close. But this wasn't the cheeky, laughing face I'd caught a glimpse of that night of the anniversary party. Something mocking yet deeply sad seeped out of it. Then I remembered the fragments of photos of Louisa I'd hidden at the bottom of my bathroom drawer among hairbrushes, razors, and lotions. Retrieving them, I began carrying them around in my trouser or jacket pocket, surreptitiously pulling them out and gazing at them.

Increasingly, as the days passed, it was Louisa's face I saw, not Penny's. I tried to imagine Louisa's life and how she'd lived it all the years since. In my mind, I saw her surrounded by a tribe of children, a smiling husband in the background. Smack up against this image came her shocked face when I told her I didn't love her, the furious incomprehension, the hostile silence that followed.

Slowly at first, then persistently, came the idea I should find out if my imaginings about her happy family life were true. I justified the thought by telling myself it would quiet my guilt at what I'd done; validate the decision to reject our love. I would return to Toronto, find Louisa, get to know her children, and sit among her happy family. She would understand and forgive what I'd done, and we might even resume a friendly relationship.

And so dreaming, I stood taller, walked purposefully, and began my research. I should add that I did neglect my work a bit, and from time to time, saw Ian's frowning face beyond the glass door of my office. He'd been promoted to vice-president, so I answered to him. I was performing below expectations. I knew it, he knew it. We were friends, so he ignored my slippage, but we both understood it couldn't go on much longer. I tried to concentrate, but my mind wasn't on numbers and percentages, or an upcoming company audit. I realized, too, that my mind wasn't on music, or rather, Penny pointed it out.

"You're not listening to anything," she said one evening when I sat at the window with no book or magazine, no recorded music playing. "You haven't touched the piano for, I don't now, weeks now." Her voice held accusation and query, a hint of worry in the latter.

I didn't know how to respond. I'd never been evasive with Penny, never mind outright lying to her, but withholding my intentions to do something of the magnitude I had in mind was probably the same thing. My lack of interest in music was mostly because of my focus on Louisa, and music hadn't been part of her world. Rarely had I mentioned to Penny that when I heard various sounds, like birdsong, they had a colour, that musical notes also transposed themselves into various shades. Why hadn't I told my wife more about something so important to me? But I knew she wouldn't have understood. And heaven help me, she might have remembered my mother and think I'd inherited a touch of craziness. Maybe I had. And so I sat there, idle, preoccupied, feeling guilty on Penny's behalf. Also, when I thought about work, on Ian's.

Back to my sleuth work on Louisa and her whereabouts: she could be anywhere, but most likely still in Toronto. She would have assumed a married name, I supposed, so I'd check first with my friends, Jack and Robbie. While in Toronto, I'd also take the opportunity to see Mom and Dad.

The next evening I mentioned casually to Penny that I planned to return to Toronto at the end of the month.

"Wait another three weeks for the March break and I'll come with you," she said in her usual brisk way.

"Well ... it's that Mom isn't quite well, and I thought it best to go sooner." As I said, I'd never lied to Penny. I stood there twisting my hands, teetering back and forth on my heels. "Just a short trip to make sure everything's okay."

Penny didn't look up but remained sifting through her students' exam papers at the kitchen table. She was still in her pajamas and had her hair tied up in a knot. A cup of coffee sat cooling on the table beside her. "Is it the old problem?"

"No, no. I think all that's gone."

"You forget. Remember how I said that when people manage to overcome their addiction or obsession, they need to find some kind of substitute? Your mom looked after three small children in her home, an after-school program, didn't she? She called the two little girls Susannah and Genevieve, and the boy Jeremy ..."

"Don't remind me," I groaned, recalling how I'd flown back home after a frantic plea from Dad that Mom was in trouble again.

"She would have to go and open this after-school daycare in our condo," Dad had said when I got there. "I didn't like it. Why would she do that? Then she began calling the kids by the names of our, you know, dead babies. At first she whispered them, then getting careless, or forgetting she was doing it, or maybe she actually believed these were her children, she spoke the names aloud. Then one day she did it with the parents. They called your mother a lunatic. They threatened to report her."

I'd been standing with my hands in my pockets opposite Dad but turned away from the pain in his eyes. Suppressing a sigh, I swivelled around to see the late-afternoon sun lance through the trees in the cemetery.

"The parents?" I asked. "What happened?"

"They took their kids away and dropped the whole subject. Now your mom's got three cats called by those … you know … those names."

Dad and I smiled at each other companionably, sadly.

Now, back in Vancouver with Penny, I said, "Even after all these years, Mom still misses the whole neighbourhood."

"But she's more or less in the same area, isn't she? She'll adjust." Penny straightened her shoulders and returned to sorting her school papers.

My guilt at my misrepresentation, well, my deliberate intent to deceive, faded at her lack of sympathy. Although she'd never had much liking for Mom and considered her odd — well, who wouldn't? — I thought her present attitude was a bit unfeeling. When I looked at her again before I got up, it seemed to me that her features were sharper, her profile tight, cold. The key signature of D minor came to mind.

That night I lay staring at the darkened window, trying to justify my lies. I realized they couldn't truly be called lies because I really did need to check on Mom and Dad. I'd never intended Louisa to re-enter my life, and she hadn't, even though I'd visited my parents in Toronto many times since moving to British Columbia. She hadn't been a major part of my thoughts or of my life until the night of our anniversary party, so thoroughly had I suppressed most thoughts and memories of her. Guilt plus heartache would do that. But could you really make a person totally disappear from your life forever? I didn't have an answer then, and began to doubt it now.

Images of one specific visit to Toronto returned to me now: the walk up Mount Pleasant Road to buy a few groceries for my parents. A figure ahead of me. The familiar walk and shape of her. She was no other than Pam Blackstock, tall, willowy, with a mass of black hair. Something hit me hard in the chest, like a blow to it, and I coughed to get my breath. I hadn't really cared much about her, only as Louisa's sister who had tried to warn me off. An urge to turn and run back the way I'd come rushed over me. Almost as a matter of life and death, I couldn't afford any reminders of that time, that part of my life. But my feet remained stuck to the sidewalk as I stared at the vanishing figure. Then, suddenly, someone else was beside her, keeping pace with her. Robbie! I recognized the way his head leaned forward, how his shoulders slouched. He was there with The Shepherdess! I watched as they linked arms, faintly heard their laughing as they continued striding northward.

Pam Blackstock and Robbie! I couldn't take it in, and my mouth had hung open at the absurdity of it. Did he also keep in touch with Louisa?

CHAPTER TWENTY-FIVE

The more urgent my need to see Louisa, the more I tried to mask my feelings, but not very successfully. After Penny's repeated questions about why I couldn't wait three weeks for the school break, after seeing the excitement in my eyes that I couldn't hide, her typical indulgence toward me ebbed. Her face closed up. When she spoke, she folded her arms and didn't look at me.

"Penny, my parents aren't getting any younger," I said, "and they deserve more help from their only son."

"But why haven't you said any of this before? And why the sudden decision to go right now?"

I had no answer. "I don't know. I guess I meant to say something and just forgot." At the heavy frown that pinched Penny's cheeks and forehead, I became defensive and added, "Do I need to tell you every detail of my life? As for Mom, what you asked about her missing children, well, I don't know how she's managed the whole business after what happened with the daycare, except for getting three cats. I've never talked to her directly about her babies, as you know, and never did. As for why I didn't tell you earlier about going back to Toronto, it's that I didn't want to bother you with it, you're ... very involved in school stuff right now."

I owed Penny. After all, she'd been the one to help me get myself together, and perhaps, after considering my mother, encouraged me to get counselling before I, like her, developed crazy ideas. Right now I thought an evening out at a nice restaurant would distract me and mollify her, so I booked a table at Five Sails at Canada Place, and at a window table no less, something hard to get with the restaurant's spectacular view of the North Shore Mountains and Burrard Inlet.

"I booked us into Five Sails for tomorrow night," I said. "It's a wonderful restaurant with lovely views that somehow we've never been to before."

Penny was surprised and pleased. She dressed in a long black skirt and plain greyish blouse. Around her neck she strung a tiny pearl necklace, and to her ears clasped pearl earrings I'd given her. It was the first time she'd ever worn them. I watched as she combed her hair, pulled it into a knot at the back, and clipped it. Watched as lightly she applied lipstick and a faint brush of colour to her cheeks. Things she rarely did.

"Beautiful," I said. "I'd take you with me anywhere."

"Okay, take me to Toronto."

"Right now, darling, tonight I'm taking you to Five Sails." I kissed both her cheeks and pulled her out the door.

"I'm surprised you haven't chosen your favourite spot on Robson Street," she said. "Why Five Sails? What's brought this on?"

"We ought to do this kind of thing more often."

"Sure, I'll go for that."

As we headed for the underground garage in our condo building, as I opened the car door for her, my image of my wife was of a lean, angular woman swathed in soft shades of lavender, quite a change from other times when she appeared in darker, streaky colours. But altogether I saw her as a woman with almost transcendental poise, calm and unruffled. Tonight her usually sharp features had softened with pleasure at the unexpected outing, and I swore she even had a bounce in her step. The key signature of F major came to mind and gave me confidence in what I had to do — not straight out lie to her, but not tell her everything about what I was about to do and why. Having to be evasive made me feel uncomfortable, and I knew that if the roles had been reversed, she would have been blunt and told me exactly what she was doing and the reasons why. And she wouldn't have cared whether I liked it or not. But then Penny would never have fallen into a relationship like the one I'd had with Louisa. She was much too sensible, too practical. *Too unromantic.* But I put that last thought aside.

∞

"Why, really, did you choose this place?' Penny asked when we were seated at our window table at Five Sails.

Before answering, I ordered martinis for both of us.

"Well?" Penny said. "Do you and your colleagues come here for business lunches?"

"No," I said. "The truth is, I've always been intrigued by this place. Maybe it's a morbid fascination. Something weird happened here once, or rather, didn't happen." I told her the story about the missing couple who had booked to dine here. "Booked this very table, but never showed up. Apparently, they were here a lot, always at this table. As you can see, it's a pretty upscale place, and the couple was well known to the manager — to all the influential people in the business world, in fact. This is where most of them come when they want to make deals, when they want to see and be seen. No one, not the police, the public, the family, has ever found an explanation for why this couple never showed up. And no one, again not family, not business associates, not friends or even the neighbours, has ever heard from them again. They didn't just not show up ever again at Five Sails. They completely vanished altogether."

"What about the Vancouver police or the RCMP?" Penny asked, eyes alight with interest. "They must have investigated. What did they say?"

"Well, periodically, they put out a call to the public to come forward with any information about the couple, but nobody has ever approached them. The police say that many people have something in their pasts they're guilty about and drop out of society perhaps to atone for it in some way …" My flow of words stopped suddenly as it hit me that this was exactly what I was doing: indulging in a need to atone for what I did to Louisa, and even more powerfully, to explain and apologize.

"Julian?" Penny's eyes were on me, curious, probing. "And what? I'm interested. Finish what you were saying."

"Yes, well …" I looked away from her. "That's the reason the police keep the incident alive with the public, and from time to time ask for the help of citizens. It might involve a crime, after all. The police hope that someone might remember a conversation, or even just a comment made long ago. Privately, most people believe these two were victims of a deal gone bad. I mean, they left in a hurry. They owned a substantial house in North Vancouver. The front door was left ajar, the alarm switched off. Their old dog was found wandering the streets and the neighbour's driveway. And worst of all, their passports were lying open on a bedside table. It's all very strange."

As I ordered a bottle of Chardonnay, and oysters for Penny — I couldn't eat the things — something hit me. Perhaps that couple had wanted to vanish and never be found, for whatever reason. Some people did, like Louisa. Well, that was how I interpreted her apparent disappearance. Part of me knew she wouldn't want to be found by me because she no doubt still hated me. With that thought, my mood soured.

Now I had to tell Penny I was going to go ahead to Toronto without her and could give no good reason why I wouldn't wait three weeks so she could come with me. Knowing I was about to displease her, knowing her rational mind would probe and probe until what I said made sense to her, I felt my face close up. She studied me, and I knew she noticed the change. Her own colours began to alter, and the soft shades that had suffused her morphed into smudged greys, then into an ominous streaked charcoal. F major became A minor.

The big thing was, I'd never lied to Penny, and she knew the story of my life except for the part about Louisa. If omission could be called lying, then I supposed I had lied. Did people, or did a couple when they got together, owe each other a full accounting of their previous lives before they'd met? Should they be completely frank? Some said yes, others said they didn't know, and still others said absolutely not. What happened in the past had nothing to do with the present relationship, though in my case it probably did.

But why should I have said anything about Louisa, since I'd blocked her out of my life and had always intended to keep it that way? And I had done so until the night of our thirtieth-anniversary party. One other thought came to me on this subject: surely, a person should be allowed some privacy. Again, surely, if everything was known about a person, there could be no mystery left. Most of us, I believed, would choose some element of mystery over understanding all the nuts and bolts that made up another person.

At the end of our seafood dinner, each of us sipping a brandy, Penny resumed our conversation about the couple who had vanished. "Some people disappear for a reason, and who knows what it might be. What do you think, Jules?"

"It sounds like you're a bit spooked by it," I said, my mind suddenly leaping to Louisa. I tried to laugh, but it didn't come out right and sounded a bit like criticism.

Penny glanced at me with what I called her analytical eyes: a narrowing of them, a piercing penetration as though searching to understand my very soul. She waited patiently for me to say something else.

I swallowed my brandy all at once. "I think we can safely leave it to the police. Listen, I want to tell you that I really do have to go back to Toronto to check on Mom and Dad and not wait until you're off. Apparently, Mom isn't well. She's acting a bit weird again. Nothing serious, but …" Penny's eyes widened in alarm, and lines appeared between her brows. "And Dad likes it when I'm there and can be a kind of emotional support for him."

"I still don't know why you had to act so suddenly, as though you've been keeping things from me." Penny kept her eyes fixed on mine.

"Sometimes I don't want to bother you with stuff like this."

"I thought a good marriage was one where the couple told each other everything."

"Do you tell me your every thought? Look, you know I've been thinking about checking on them for some time but didn't want to tell you until I'd decided for sure."

"Okay." But Penny's frown deepened. "If you've finished your drink, let's go. The sky's getting dark and we're probably in for a storm." The evening for her was over. She stood up and signalled to the waiter. "I'll pay."

As we walked to the car, a rainstorm broke over us. Lifting my face to feel the rain, I saw the sky rip open and bolts of purple and angry green dart at us, sharp enough to tear through our clothes.

"Run!" I yelled at Penny with real fear.

CHAPTER TWENTY-SIX

Penny and I moved around each other carefully during the two weeks before I flew to Toronto. A few evenings after another small dinner party, I fell asleep in my chair by the window. In my mind, I was back with Louisa in the long grass outside the Church of the Transfiguration off Mount Pleasant Road. "I'm going to kiss you," Louisa said as she leaned over me, teasing me.

I lingered in that kiss, tasting it, when I heard a faint clatter and tinkle of glass, of background music, the knocking of bottles against one another, water running. And then someone was breathing in my face, pulling on my arms. A voice, not Louisa's, spoke softly but urgently in my ear. I opened my eyes to see Penny leaning over me, telling me to wake up. Sprawled in the armchair against the south-facing living room wall, she appeared as an insubstantial shadow in the pool of late-afternoon sunshine filtering through the window. *I'm going to kiss you* became mixed up with *Julian, wake up, wake up! Are you sick? What is it? What's wrong with you?*

Being abruptly yanked out of one life and into another was a wrenching experience. Drifting across my face tumbled the cloud of Penny's light hair. Her voice in my ear, strained and hollow, again urged me to wake up, get up. I was a puppet jerked on the strings of wild emotions, only suddenly to be let go. I looked at her, at the beads of sweat glistening on her upper lip, the alarm that blanched her face. Remnants of the recent dinner party were all around me — empty wine and beer bottles, scraps of congealing food on plates scattered on countertops and stools — and I registered that Penny had been wiping away an evening's excess.

All the vivid images and outsize emotions were now fairy dust, as if by the wave of a witch's wand they'd been replaced by this thin, unshaped woman bending over me with coffee-laden breath.

"I think I had a bit too much to drink, that's all," I said. "I was feeling a bit queasy before dinner. Right now I just need some air and then I'll be back to help you finish cleaning up."

"But, Jules, look at you. You're exhausted."

I got up, anyway, and after a quick squeeze of her arm, left the apartment, annoyed at being dragged out of a period of my life that suddenly, alarmingly, had begun to threaten my present one. On a bench under a plane tree, I contemplated the clear blue-green sky. The air felt chillier, and I pulled my nylon jacket tighter across my chest. Planting my feet among fallen leaves, I thought how memories of the past loomed larger as we got older, how they had a powerful hold on our emotions that often ran much deeper than more recent ones. How heavily our impressionable years were inscribed in them, how impossible it was to erase them. Deliberately, I'd locked Louisa away so that she didn't exist for me, not in all the years since. Or so I'd thought. Having been let loose — all because of that anniversary party and those wretched photos — she'd rocketed back more powerfully than ever.

As people ambled by me seemingly aimless, I tried to focus my thoughts. My decision to revisit my past life became more pressing. And so I summoned it, thinking that was the only way to put it to rest, to see it for what it had been: a teenage schoolboy crush. Back in my present life, still under the plane tree with the wind noisily tossing leaves, with people walking by shouldering bags of groceries, I decided that whenever I got the chance, I'd definitely allow myself to finish that journey to my parents' old house.

On the weekends, pretending I had shopping to do or a library to visit, I took myself off into the gloom of small churches, to quiet corners of coffee bars, to park benches overlooking Lost Lagoon at the entrance to Stanley Park, hoping to lose myself in those early years. As I fixed my mind on myself as a boy, a teenager, a young man, I felt the boundaries of myself blur, even dissolve. I'd had that experience before — in Mount Pleasant Cemetery when I found a marker, first with Genevieve's name, birth, and death on it, then one for Susannah, labelled "Sus." Also when I saw Louisa arm in arm with Leon, I'd freaked out, had a meltdown. Now I accepted these feelings more calmly as part of who I was and how I reacted to difficult things.

During lunch and after work, I frequented local coffee shops, sometimes a bar. With a book or magazine propped in front of me, pretending to read it, again I retreated to my younger years. I had a problem to be solved. I needed time alone to think, to put pieces of my life together to make sense of them. Like a mathematical equation or an arithmetical problem, I searched for solutions so I could arrive at a conclusion. I took longer lunches, left work earlier, sat behind my desk at work, but did little. Ian started dropping by my office. He'd sit on the edge of my desk and chat about sports, upcoming concerts, then abruptly ask if anything was wrong with me, was I well.

Surprised, disconcerted, I'd say I was fine, that nothing was wrong.

He'd stand, stare at me for a moment, say, "Okay," then leave.

Disjointed in time and space, I'd continue to sit and gaze

at everything and nothing in my office until I had to get out of there, to be anywhere but at work or at home.

Memories of my early years came to me in jagged bursts, like arrows piercing the life I'd so carefully set up and lived all the years since. One minute I was on Denman Street on my way to the supermarket and passing the Death by Chocolate store in Vancouver's West End. In another I was behind my desk on Howe Street with Ian more frequently coming by to ask me pointed questions about my health and home life. Penny's eyes were on me, worried, and suddenly I was swinging up Mount Pleasant Road on my bike after work, first to stop in at home, then off to a date with Louisa.

One morning I walked into the office to find an envelope on my desk addressed to me. It was handwritten in tight, scrawling letters with a Toronto postmark. I'd meant to open it later, but pushed it into a heap of other unopened mail and forgot it.

CHAPTER TWENTY-SEVEN

My discomfort and unhappiness in lying to my wife didn't stop me from immediately beginning my investigation into finding Louisa. In my heart, I knew I didn't need to go to Toronto and could easily discover what I wanted to know from Vancouver. But that wasn't enough. I was on a mission, lit up inside by some vast emotion. I needed to redefine myself. I had to see Louisa, to find out about her life for myself.

I called Mom and Dad to say I had a few days off and was flying over. "Do you still have enough room for me to stay with you?"

"The spare room is always yours, dear Julian," Mom said. "We bought a new bed for it, a chair, and a nice dresser for your clothes." My mood brightened at how normal she sounded, how she really did mean the "dear Julian" part. And nothing about the babies.

The flight I booked would leave in three days' time. I went to the office early the next two days, trying to concentrate on work in an attempt to make up for my slacking off. Sometimes I stayed late and Ian no longer passed by to check on me. But my staying late created problems with Penny. She thought I was avoiding her, and true to her nature, didn't say anything, only observed me until she felt she understood, or not understanding, just came straight out with what was on her mind.

"You owe me," she said the second evening when I slid in the door at close to eight.

I could hear her at the piano, how she stopped when she heard my key in the lock.

She got up, went to the fridge, retrieved a bottle of white wine, and poured herself a full glass. Standing in the middle of the living room, a tight expression on her face, she said, "First, you spring on me that you're going off to Toronto with no good explanation for why you have to go right now, then you suddenly start running off early to the office and staying late, all with no explanation." She drank half her glass of wine in one gulp while staring at me over its rim. "Before I was worried about you and your work because you seemed to be slacking, now you've become all conscientious and staying at the office all hours — or do you? What's changed?"

"I already told you why I have to go to Toronto. About work, we didn't have a lot coming in because we'd lost a few clients. Now it's picking up, and Ian has piled stuff on me."

"Your dinner's in the oven," she said, and walked into the bedroom.

I felt sorry for her. Guilty, too, but my feelings didn't — couldn't — change anything. The idea of Louisa remained fixed in my subconscious. At night dreams came at me that bordered on nightmares: Louisa as a ghostly figure sliding along the bedroom walls in the same way my phantom siblings had once done. Then her face slamming into mine, red and furious. Her voice, when I heard it, was at times teasing, laughing, then accusing.

You're such a square, did you know that? That was the laughing voice. The teasing one said: *You're an original, a singular fellow, Julian. I don't believe the likes of you will ever be seen again.*

Shh, shh, I whispered until another voice joined the first.

"Who on earth are you shushing in your sleep, Jules?"

Penny's voice was in my ear, her wispy hair in my face.

"Nobody! I wasn't saying anything."

I started daydreaming more, listening for Louisa's voice, hearing her words, some of them coming to me bright and unpolished, as though saved up especially for me. Those times my heart swelled as if it would burst through my chest. In my dreams, I became a giant striding the world. At work I slacked off again, sitting behind my desk lost in dreams, staring at nothing. One morning Amanda, my secretary, knocked on my office door and pointed at the pile of unopened mail on my desk. "Is there anything in that pile I should deal with while you're gone?" she asked in her typically timid voice.

I glanced at the neat stack. "I'll take a quick look and let you know."

She bobbed out the door, and I closed it, then picked through the pile until an envelope addressed to me in thin, spidery handwriting jumped out. I slid it open and read:

Yo cousin. You'll be surprised to get this, but you shouldn't. Take it serious. I need cash, and fast. You're the one who got it all. For starters you got Uncle Albert's apartment. What did you do with it — sell it? Whatever, I figure you've got the cash. Fifty thou would do for now. Send a cheque at once to Post Office Box 1672 … If I don't get it by April 17, I'll have to tell your wifey what you've been keeping from her. I know where you live. She might be real interested in what you did to a poor innocent girl before you met her.

                                  Yo-ho, Steve.

A stone lodged somewhere inside me, cold and hard. I stared out the window at a sky that had been blue last time

I looked but had darkened to brackish brown, exactly the colour of Steve's eyes. My heart beat hard against my chest and my thoughts raced. Could Steve be serious? How would he know I hadn't told Penny about Louisa? And how much would she care if she knew? Hearing it from Steve, I guessed. Her image came to me, cold and snappy as I imagined what she'd say.

"Why didn't you tell me, Jules?"

"I ... well, it was way in the past and had nothing to do with us."

We'd have the discussion again about privacy, argue whether a person needed to know all the details of another person's life upon entering a relationship. Surely, it wasn't relevant. To her, something like this would be.

"What else have you kept from me?" she'd ask.

What I did know for sure was that if the roles were reversed, Penny would have told me. But then she'd never have allowed herself to become so embroiled with the male equivalent of Louisa, if ever there could be such a person.

I slumped in my desk chair, moodily studying my hands, in particular the wedding band shining on my ring finger. More lying to Penny. I'd have to withdraw the money from my personal account — Penny and I pooled our incomes for all household and travel expenses but kept separate accounts for personal stuff. Fifty thousand dollars! Would Steve really follow through? If he was truly desperate, I knew he would.

He sounded as if he was really in trouble.

Drugs probably.

I did get everything.

He got nothing.

It wasn't fair to him, regardless of what kind of a person he was, or had been. And what kind of chance had he had?

My thoughts churned until, feeling dizzy, I rested my

head on the desk. Suddenly, there was a rap on the door, and Ian walked in.

"Julian …" His voice was formal, eyes refusing to meet mine. "We need to have a talk when you return from Toronto." Then he turned and left.

At the end of the workday I wandered the streets of downtown Vancouver, trying to sort out what to do. It was late when I slid my key in the door at home, but I'd made a decision. I wouldn't send Steve a cheque in the mail but would take a chequebook with me and try to find him, see how I could help him.

As for Louisa, my plan was simply to find out if she was happily married and had a bunch of children … well, at least one. I told myself I'd be satisfied to know this. Then I could forget her and get on with my life. But unable to control my fantasies, I again imagined having some kind of relationship with her. We would become friends, soulmates. It would make worthwhile all the pain and sacrifice both of us had made.

CHAPTER TWENTY-EIGHT

I flew on the red-eye, leaving a rainy, overcast Vancouver and arriving in Toronto on an early Sunday morning that was cool and clear. The city's deciduous trees hadn't yet sprung their new leaves, but still the view was pretty spectacular from the air. It seemed surreal to jet from mountains and sea, from my job on busy Howe Street in Vancouver, to be deposited among Toronto's high-rises and shadowy ravines. The atmosphere struck me as different here, the feel of the city and its people, too: fast, crowded, choked, and sprawling.

I rented a car at the airport and decided Jack would be my first contact, since he might be the one to know Louisa's whereabouts. Although it was early in the day, Jack probably wouldn't mind an impromptu visit.

∞

"Hey, fella, still got your head stuck in the back of a piano?"

I stood with Jack in his driveway in the leafy suburb of Don Mills. His red hair had thinned and lost its bright colour. His late-middle-aged whiskered face smiled ear to ear as we talked about his life, work, and kids. Of mine I said little other than: "No, I didn't pursue the actuarial thing but got myself a good job at a firm called Fairbanks & Co., a management position, in fact." That was a moment of pride.

"Hey, how's Robbie?" I asked. "I never hear from him, or anything about him. What's he up to?"

"Ah, yes, Robbie. You're in for a surprise. You ready for this?"

"Okay … what?"

"He and Pam Blackstock got together, quite a long time ago, in fact." Jack grinned at me as though this was a big joke, but his eyes were on me, intent. Why should I react? What was it to me? But the news felt strange, something about it not right.

"You know what I think?" Jack began. "That girl Pam was after *you*. And since she couldn't get you, she went after someone close to you — our Robbie."

"Are … are they happy? Do they have any kids?"

"Kids? Why do you ask?"

"Just, I don't know." I shrugged it off. It — they — belonged to another life that now had nothing to do with mine. Then, not able to hold back any longer about my real purpose in being here, I came out with it. "Hey, speaking of Pam, do you know what happened to her sister, Louisa?" I kicked a loose stone on the path with my foot and looked away from Jack.

He seemed surprised, then frowned. "Oh, her …" His eyes were on me. "Yes, Louisa. I heard she went to George Brown for some arts program. Last I heard, from Leon of all people — put your hands down! — she got a job at the University of Toronto's Faculty Club, but I can't tell you for sure what she does there. Manager maybe? Is she married? Once maybe, but not anymore that I heard. Kids — I dunno." After a pause, he added, "Jules, why do you want to know? Whatever was between the two of you, wasn't it all over a long time ago?"

"Just curious," I said lightly. As we walked together indoors for coffee, I changed the subject, asking instead about other old schoolmates. I could scarcely concentrate, dumbfounded about Louisa. Working at the Faculty Club! She'd

182 CAROLYN TAYLOR-WATTS

never harboured an ambition for business management that I knew, and I certainly couldn't picture it. The only ambition she'd admitted to was painting and making the world — and herself — beautiful. How then could she achieve and maintain a job like that and raise a bunch of kids?

Before beginning a search for her, I sat in my rental car, then decided that first I'd take a trip down memory lane. People said you started to take sentimental journeys into your past or looked over your shoulder at where you'd been when you were in your fifties. Was it simple nostalgia or a sort of accounting of where you'd been and what you'd achieved?

I recalled I'd done something similar the night of our thirtieth-anniversary party when I made a tally of the pluses and minuses of my life to that date. Whatever my reasons now, I went cruising up and down Mount Pleasant Road and along Merton Street. Idly, I watched people amble here and there, enter local shops, and stroll out again. Then, suddenly, there was Steve! A shadow at first, solidifying eventually, stolid, heavy. Jolted, I stared. But was it him? I looked again. No, not unless he'd straightened up and walked with his head held high. I'd completely forgotten about him and his threat. After that, I imagined I saw him everywhere, but perhaps I was feeling guilty and merely seeing things.

Recovering from that shock, I drove down Mount Pleasant to my old house. Many things had changed. George's Trains had vanished. At the corner of Mount Pleasant and Merton, Dominion Coal and Wood had been levelled, disappeared as though it had never been. From its ashes, a high-rise was emerging. I thought about change, how it would continue to slip along imperceptibly, inexorably, until the landscape of my childhood would be unrecognizable. Had I become unrecognizable? Had Louisa?

Soon I was at our old house. I hadn't seen it since Mom and Dad had sold it and moved into their condo. It was curious that most people when they moved remained in the area of the city they were familiar with, even if wasn't convenient for them anymore. Our old house had a new coat of paint and new front steps. A paved driveway covered the front garden, and I hoped Mom hadn't come back to see that her gladioli and dahlias had been vanquished under concrete, under the wheels of a Chevrolet. All the other houses remained the same — a mix of styles, shapes, and sizes that were noteworthy but didn't add up to a coherent streetscape.

I idled in front of the house on the opposite side of the street, vaguely aware of a sense of absence within and surrounding it, something I'd scarcely noticed before, or had buried in my subconscious while living there. Its colours were a blur of shadowy greens and greys. With the car windows open, I listened for baby cries, for lullabies to float from the upstairs windows, for the fluttering of curtains, for the shadows of ghosts to glide along its outside walls. But a sense of nothingness hung over the house, a pall of bland pink-beige. With relief, together with a sense of having lost something, I drove away. If only my old memories of Louisa could be so simply dealt with. "But I don't want to be rid of them!" I cried out to the empty street.

My next destination was my parents' condo. Because of Mom's history, I was sorry they'd chosen a place that overlooked Mount Pleasant Cemetery, but I liked its layout, especially its mezzanine level. I wouldn't have had it painted white throughout, but it was clean and unambiguous, no shadows. There was only one spare bedroom and so no space for Mom's three dead children. At least that was what I hoped. Now I was about to find out what she'd done after the disastrous after-school daycare program she'd run. Such a powerful illusion, fixation, or whatever it might be called, surely had to be replaced by something else, as Penny had said. As I entered through the open door of the condo and into the kitchen, I passed by the spare bedroom. Its door stood half open, but no baby smells, no nursery rhymes, drifted from it. *Whew!*

After we gave each other an awkward hug, I stood back and regarded Mom. She'd begun wearing pantsuits, had allowed her hair to fall in a pageboy style around her face, and had given it a new ash-blond colour. This was a new mother!

Dad, when he appeared from the bedroom, looked good, too. Hearty in his welcome, happy in his new home, he joked, "No upkeep. It's an easy life now."

He got me a mug of coffee while Mom put egg salad sandwiches and muffins on the table. The early-afternoon sunlight streamed through the skylight above the second-floor mezzanine into the dining room, spangling it with whites and golds. I all but held my breath as the three of us sat at the old dining table, relaxed, happy to be in one another's company. But I avoided glancing at the hallway to the half-open door of the spare bedroom. Whatever was in there could wait.

Dad insisted on knowing all the details of my life and Penny's in Canada's most beautiful city. His eyes were bright and full of anticipation to hear about our time "out there."

I was about to launch into a rosy account of our lives when the front door opened to a grey-haired, slightly stooping man. Startled at the intrusion, I glanced up to see Uncle Robert. At least two decades must have passed since I'd last seen him, and now I hardly recognized him.

He said a perfunctory hello to Mom and Dad, then turned and considered me intently. "Ha, the young fellow's here. But not so young anymore, I suppose, like all of us. Some do it better than others, eh?" His eyes bored into mine as he moved forward to hold out a hand. "Have you forgotten your Uncle Robert already? No substitute for your beloved Uncle Albert, eh?"

I didn't like the way he stared at me, at the angry half-smile on his face. Recalling the whispers about him, I concluded he was a relative no one particularly wanted around.

"*The* young fellow?" I said, and was about to say more when Mom interrupted.

"Robert, there's coffee in the kitchen if you want. Help yourself."

Dad spread his hands. "Were we expecting you, Rob?"

Uncle Robert put his hands on his hips. "Can't your brother just drop in to see his family? To see your son?"

Into the silence, Mom said, "Penelope's been phoning you, Jules. She expected you to call as soon as you arrived." She raised her pencilled brows in inquiry. "In the bedroom where you'll be sleeping, there's a phone. You can call her from there." She regarded me for a moment as though weighing something, then turned to Uncle Robert. "I suppose you'll want lunch?" Then she got up to pour her brother-in-law a mug of coffee.

I should have phoned Penny. But now I couldn't even summon the shape of her. "I'll call her later," I said.

Over lunch, ignoring Uncle Robert who kept staring at me, I launched into a description of my position at Fairbanks & Co., and about Penny's ascent to vice-principal at a West End elementary school.

Before I could add any more details to satisfy Mom, she interrupted me, her voice a bit breathless, "And you're playing the piano, still practising hard? Have you got yourself a position in the concert halls or the symphony yet?"

"Oh, Mom! It takes years and years, and they look for younger talent. I'm in my fifties, you know." To soften her disappointment, I added, "I do play at studios here and there, and … occasionally at a nightclub." I hesitated revealing this last bit of information, expecting she would disapprove. But she was overwhelmed by an old sense of defeat. Not only was I not a soloist in an orchestra, I held no position there at all.

Her shoulders drooped, and the light went out of her eyes. "That's lovely, dear," was all she said, and the colours that had been evoked by her voice dimmed.

"You making lots of money?" Uncle Robert had his mug to his lips. "You got a mighty good start from your Uncle Albert, and I'm sure you're getting even richer out there."

The silence stretched like a chasm between us. To me, the white walls of the dining room darkened into the same colours evoked by Uncle Robert's voice.

"I'm not sure what you're saying," I began. "I did get a start from Uncle Albert way back —"

"And my boy got nothing!" Uncle Robert growled.

Mom stood poised over the table, a tea towel in her hand. Now she began wringing it.

Dad pushed back his chair and stood. "Whatever Steve's done with his life has nothing to do with Julian."

"No? You owe him," Uncle Robert spat. "You owe my son — all of you! I say Julian better pay up!"

"Why are you bringing this up now?" Dad demanded.

I knew. Steve was in trouble and needed money fast. My throat was dry. Hoarsely, I asked, "Uncle Robert, what about Steve? What's he doing ... and where is he — in Toronto?"

"Ah, you're so interested all of a sudden. Planning to share your spoils with him, after all?" At the sneer in his voice, I saw smudged colours swirl in the air around him.

"Robert!" Mom picked up the tea towel lying in her lap and shook it in his face. "How *can* you?"

"Stop it, all of you!" Dad squared his shoulders and stared hard at Uncle Robert.

"If you want to give my son a share of your riches, you can give it to me," Uncle Robert said. "You know where I live. I'll pass it on to my boy." He reached for a slice of chocolate cake before heading for the door.

"Wait!" Jumping up, I almost knocked over my chair. "Can you give me Steve's address or phone number?"

Uncle Robert halted with his hand on the doorknob. Not expecting this, looking wary, he took a ballpoint pen from his shirt pocket, a scrap of paper from another, scribbled an address on it, and tossed it to me. The next moment he was gone.

"I do feel guilty about Steve," I said when the door slammed behind him. "I felt guilty back then. I always thought he should've inherited something from Uncle Albert."

Dad muttered that none of that had anything to do with us, but I interrupted him.

"What's *with* Uncle Robert, anyway? Did he know I was going to be here? Did he really expect me to hand over half of Uncle Arthur's inheritance to Steve after all this time and just like that? Well, maybe I should have given him at least some of it." An image of Steve came to me then, of the two of us clowning around in the cemetery when we were boys, Steve's exuberance and delight in that innocent world of our childhood.

Then I noticed Dad was giving me a look that said: "Why are you doing this?"

"Do you see much of him?" I persisted, avoiding my parents' puzzled eyes on me.

"No," Dad said. "He and your Aunt Lindy are moving back from Niagara Falls. I guess he's looking for a place." Dad told me all this tonelessly without pleasure or displeasure.

"Do you really know nothing about Steve?"

"No," Mom said. She was still wringing the tea towel. "But I don't think things are so good. We believe Steve's back taking drugs. I hope to God he's not dealing them!"

"And after all the rehab he went through — such a waste," Dad grumbled.

Drugs! Of course! It had always stared me in the face, always been in the back of my mind. Those few times I'd spent with Steve, his body language, his facial expressions, his voice when he spoke — at the memory of it all I saw him suffused in jagged streaks of red. Upset, not knowing what my obligations to him might be, what to do about his blackmailing of me, I got up and paced the elongated living room. "I have to phone Penny," I finally said, and moved slowly toward the spare bedroom.

I approached it, my heart hammering. Gingerly, I pushed open the door and switched on the light. A dozen pairs of eyes stared back at me, and I fell back against the wall, suppressing a groan. Whatever I'd imagined, it wasn't this! Some of the pairs of eyes were wide open, others closed. A dozen or more faces smiled, frowned, puckered, gaped. The eyes upon me were blue, brown, hazel, green. Girl dolls in flouncy dresses, boy dolls in blue suits. All stood upright on shelves lining the back wall. Something about the blond one in the middle row struck me: Genevieve — that was it! Exactly like the snapshot taken of her at five months. The bedroom walls folded in on me, and I fell to the floor, still gazing up at the replica of my dead sister. Her tiny mouth opened, and I glimpsed a row of baby teeth, behind them, a hideous emptiness. Then she winked at me. Hyperventilating at the sheer horror of it, I struggled to get up and out of there, only to slide to the floor again. A chill shot all the way down my spine. *Stop! Stop!* I cried out silently. *You're only a doll! You're all just stupid dolls!*

Time became an abstract notion as I lay on the bare floor, my eyes closed. When a measure of composure returned, I glanced up, and all the doll faces swam together. Lurching to my feet, I grabbed the corner of a white dresser to prevent myself from collapsing once more. There, beside it, lay three wooden doll beds, two girl dolls and one boy doll cradled within them, crocheted blankets neatly arranged around them. The girls had blond hair, the boy, neatly cut brown locks. Other than a single adult bed and a small bookshelf, that was all there was in the room. No plaster casts of baby clothing. No accoutrements of the kind Mom had had in the phantom siblings' bedrooms in our old house. So this was Mom's substitute for her phantom babies. I decided that, however it had shocked me, it was certainly an improvement, and released a long-held breath.

I was about to pick up the phone to call Penny when a shadow appeared in the doorway — Mom suddenly looking small, shrivelled, her face bloodless. Her eyes flicked to the dolls, then locked on mine. Just as suddenly as she'd appeared, she turned and walked away. Nothing was ever said about the dolls.

Only later did I learn that Mom had also developed new hobbies: playing bridge with a few of the old neighbours; knitting and sewing for their grandchildren, seemingly not bitter at having none of her own. I guessed that was how she made up for it. Apart from the dolls, and however she talked to them, I could hear her telling her friends: "My son has an important job in a big accounting firm on Howe Street in Vancouver. He hobnobs with high-flying corporate types — you know the kind. Penelope, my daughter-in-law, is one of the important people in education and has just been promoted to school vice-principal. And, you know, they socialize with many well-to-do people, even some in government."

What pleased me was that Dad had joined a croquet club at the north end of Mount Pleasant Road and had made a few friends there.

"You look more and more like your Uncle Albert," Mom

said just before I left to run some errands. Playfully, she pulled on my protruding ears, ran a finger across my wide forehead — wider still since my hairline had begun to recede. "I tell my friends you're a rich man, what with your working on upscale Howe Street and dining on Robson Street, going about with all the millionaires and important people on it."

Dear Mom. The taut lines in her face had relaxed, and I believed there were two reasons for that: she had finally come to terms with her lack of children and grandchildren, and had mostly put all her dead children to rest. Her substitution had taken a benign form — a room full of dolls. In her own particular way, she was proud of me and could now do a little boasting to her friends.

Speaking of moving on, I thought when I returned from my errands, it was time for me to do what I'd come here for — find Louisa. A plummeting sensation, mingled with heart-thumping excitement, warred in my chest. And there was also the business with Steve. Again, I conjured him and the way he'd been, the two of us as kids jousting, fooling around in the cemetery, in the park, on the tennis courts. That night, before I fell dead tired into my bed in the room among the dolls, I composed a letter to him, saying I was happy to share some of Uncle Albert's money gained through the sale of his apartment, that I would like to meet with him and hand it over personally. Maybe we could have lunch. I also told him to phone me next evening and gave him a number.

CHAPTER TWENTY-NINE

My priority the next day was to mail my letter to Steve. I drove first to the post office for an envelope and stamp, watched my letter slide through the mailbox, and felt a moment of weightlessness, freedom from vague, decades-long guilt.

Next, I drove to Louisa's old home, cruising past it along Hillsdale Avenue. I parked on the opposite side to it, slouched low in my seat, and studied the small home that had bulged with all the children in it, all of whom would be grown up by now. A deep sigh rose in my throat. The house with all its wooden window ledges needed paint. Also its front steps. The lawns, rusting bikes abandoned on it, needed mowing. Through an open window, I heard someone laugh, then voices. Old English folk music drifted from it.

Two elderly women exited the front door, bent over the front porch railing, and chatted. An old man with a crown of white hair came out behind them and stared in front of him. None of them were people from my past, or from Louisa's, evidence that her family no longer lived here. On impulse I got out of the car, approached the women, and asked, "Do you know where the previous family — the Blackstocks — moved to? The family with a lot of children?"

Both women shrugged. "No," one of them said. "We bought the house from a middle-aged couple with no children. The family you speak of must have sold to that couple."

I left the car and ambled out to Mount Pleasant Road and all the way to the tennis courts. Suddenly, I spotted a fellow who looked like Steve: the short neck, square shoulders, awkward gait. He sauntered into the park above the tennis courts, heading toward a bench. I looked again. It wasn't Steve. *Damn, I'm hallucinating. He's a phantom of my guilty mind.*

The courts were empty, since it was still early spring. The nets sagged, and scattered puddles added to a general sense of neglect. Farther up, I saw that the restaurant and bar opposite, The Longest Yard, remained. The Baptist church also stood solid and impervious to the changes around it.

I returned to the car, and after driving farther north, parked near the school and got out to begin a restless stroll up and down the sidewalks. In among ragged hedges, early violets and snowdrops struggled up through the bare ground. Rain began to fall as people passed by me with pale, dazed expressions. As always, Toronto had just come through a bitter winter that seemed reluctant to leave.

Just north of Eglinton, I gazed up at my old school and didn't see a figure on a park bench, his legs sticking into the middle of the pavement. I tripped and almost fell over them.

"What the hell!" I yelped.

I stared down at him. The fellow was dressed in shabby jeans, an open nylon jacket over a stained T-shirt, certainly not warm enough for the chilly spring day. His head had been nodding drowsily on his chest, and I supposed him to be a homeless drunk sleeping off his booze in the afternoon.

The fellow slowly lifted his head, and though the eyes that were raised to me were dull and confused, though lank brown hair half covered his face, I recognized him: my old high school nemesis, Leon, the class bully.

"Leon! Dear God! Is that really you?" I couldn't believe my eyes. "Are you all right?" But I didn't really care if he was or wasn't. "Are you all right?" I repeated, amazed, curious.

His head jerked again, and his eyes cleared as he focused. "Yeah, I know you, don't I?"

An ugly sneer had already twisted his lips. I could scarcely believe my eyes, hardly take in the knowledge of what he had become — a drunk on a park bench in the middle of the day, and probably homeless. Conflicting feelings of astonishment, disgust, and pity flooded me, mingled with a fleeting sense that a kind of justice had been accomplished, one he had exacted on himself.

I turned away, remembering all too well the terror and humiliation Leon had inflicted on me, how after I punched him onto the sidewalk with a well-placed blow in defence of Louisa, I'd experienced real fear, knowing it was only a matter of time before he came for me, to beat me up with all the force his hatred could inspire. Despite his present deteriorated state, I saw old hostility burning in his face, like a mask of black ice. Then, abruptly, he held out a hand, palm upward. "Got a spare loonie, mister?" As he looked up at me one final time with what I guessed was a long-practised expression — that of a beaten dog — I thought that some people did indeed bite the dust, and here sat one of the most deserving.

∞

Jack had mentioned the University of Toronto's Faculty Club as the place he thought Louisa worked, had even suggested she might be its manager. That didn't fit with anything I knew about her, but how well had I really known her? Of course, she would have grown up and changed, would obviously have, or have had, a career, would have married and had children. Well, at least one, which might vindicate what I'd done.

It was late afternoon when I walked along Willcocks

Street toward the Faculty Club, pondering the destructive emotion that was guilt. We all had regrets, guilt about the things we'd done. My most immediate one was about Mom and how I'd treated her. I should have been more sympathetic, more understanding, tried harder to please her and do the things I knew would have made her proud, become a doctor, a lawyer, a *concert pianist*! As for what I'd done to Louisa, it had to be one of the cruellest things one person could do to another. Imagining her to be a still-beautiful woman who had matured, held an important job, married a nice husband, and had some children helped a little. Maybe she didn't even recall what I'd done. Then a thought struck me: would she even remember me? A barrage of complicated feelings assailed me, and I raked my hands through my thinning hair.

I continued toward the Faculty Club. The muscles in my neck were tight, my jaw tense, and my heart raced so madly that I felt faint. Something ugly was building inside me, a vision of myself as a monster, a beast, a man who could never atone for what he'd done. Then the notion vanished, replaced with an image of Louisa walking arm in arm with me, laughing, teasing me, the two of us best friends and soulmates. What had happened all those years ago had never occurred.

I took in a few deep breaths, and in an attempt to relax, scuffed the remnants of last year's autumn leaves as I walked, admiring the shapes they assumed. I listened for sounds of the trees preparing to burst into new life, for the click of boots on the pavement, for all the colours created by the expected harmonies. But I was too tight within myself, too cold; I heard and saw nothing.

Next I tried to create the scenario for our meeting. In my mind, we fell into each other's arms. We laughed and cried. She understood why I'd done what I had. It was because I'd loved her and wanted her to have what all women wanted — kids. I told her we could be friends, share each other's lives a little bit; care about each other. I'd meet her husband and tell him how lucky he was — no, that wouldn't do if he was the jealous type. One day, even, I'd introduce her to Penny and we would all be friends. And so my thoughts ran on.

Thinking about coming upon Louisa by surprise, I slipped through the large front door to the building that housed the Faculty Club, a Georgian Revival, not striking from the outside but with a beautiful interior. I stood at the entrance to the heavily brocaded main room, its fireplace throwing up a warm glow in a subdued light. A few people sat here and there reading. I headed along the hall toward the dining room, a large expanse that had hosted many thousands of elegant dinners, weddings, birthday parties, celebrations of all kinds. Whisperings from past events, and the people who had filled it, echoed from its high panelled walls. A glance through the doors revealed suited men bent toward one another in conversation. I ventured back along the hallway and slipped downstairs to the pub. At a table I ordered a drink. I would calm myself and then ask about Louisa. In the dim light, I saw figures leaning toward one another in desultory conversation.

Someone laughed, a high-pitched tinkling, and shock ripped through me. That laugh! I jumped up, knocking my glass to the floor. I knew that laugh! I couldn't breathe and sank heavily back into the chair. With a rush of saliva almost choking me, I tried to catch my breath, all the while looking wildly about. The low light made it hard to see anything properly. In a far corner, a woman stood beside a table where two men dined. She was short, even in her platform shoes. Her skirt was slit up the side, revealing the spreading flesh of her calves and thighs. My eyes travelled farther to her plump arms, one elbow resting on the table. Her breasts spilled from a low-cut, blow-away kind of thing that was her blouse.

Wait! It just couldn't be! Fascinated, appalled, I turned to stare again, a kind of sickness rising inside me. This woman, this grown-old Louisa but still dressing and acting like a flirty teenager, laid a hand on one man's shoulder and with the other flipped her long, brittle-looking bleached hair over her shoulder. How well I knew that gesture! Again, came that laugh.

My thoughts raced. This then was the shrine of my passion, of my hero-worship, of my bitter regrets — Louisa, an old woman now. Well, not old but a train wreck. Unbelievably, she still thought of herself as a sexy young girl who could seduce any fellow without even trying. The astonishment I felt was mixed with relief that I immediately identified as a momentary abatement of my guilt, disbelief, and pity. She still thought of herself as a teenager, *as a seductress*! And she still acted like one. How was it possible?

My elbows on the table, head in my hands, I hunched there, a hard pain in my heart as though a stone had lodged in it. How could she not have grown up at all? How could she look at herself and believe she was still that cute young girl? People changed as they got older, and not just physically. Or did they? An image of Leon suddenly came to me. A bully. A coward. A loser. But what were the forces that influenced him? And maybe the way he'd been and still was wasn't really his fault.

By that logic, Louisa's behaviour and appearance wasn't her fault, either. I knew some of the background that had shaped her, the anonymity in her large family. Overlooked, even ignored, invisible in other words. And so she'd set out to build a stage for herself to be noticed. But surely people couldn't blame their environments all their lives; surely, they could take some responsibility. My thoughts flowed in this vein until I saw the woman who looked like Louisa straighten. She glanced around the room, and her eyes caught mine, but without recognition. Again, she flicked her long hair, pouted her thick pink lips, then formed them into a half-smile.

"Louisa!" I cried out, but my voice came out as a whisper. "It's Julian — remember me?" Then, with a flash of bitterness, I saw myself also as an old man, saw the pair of us, sweethearts and lovers, gnarled and distorted by time, by overlays of anger, miscommunication, and betrayal. Forgetting my purpose in seeking her, confused and even panicky because I didn't know what I should do now, I got up stiffly. About to leave for the stairs, I found myself heading toward her, repeating in a voice loud enough for her to hear, "Louisa! It's me, Julian."

Her eyes darted around, focusing and refocusing. She took a few steps toward me, approached closer, and said slowly, "I don't know you, do I?" As soon as she'd spoken, I saw her flash of recognition. Her mouth twisted, distorting the still-pretty features, only to disappear in the next instant.

We regarded each other, only a few feet of space between us, but universes apart — more than thirty-five years after that last time. A hard, metallic glint appeared in her eyes. The lines on her face deepened, became harsh, and when I took in the whole wreck of her, I wondered if it was because of what I'd done to her, or because of the life she'd chosen.

"I'm at work," she said, her voice flat, cold. "I'm a waitress here. I don't know what you've got to say to me. I can't think of anything to say to you." Her whole demeanour was of someone bored, not wanting to be bothered with any exchange.

A waitress! Like me, she was in her mid-fifties but waited on tables in a basement pub. I watched as she moved among the tables, her legs wobbling on platform shoes, her waist bulging beyond the band of her skirt. The old swinging walk was diminished, I supposed by arthritis, but still she swung her long, bleached hair, now touched with grey roots, swished and flicked it over her shoulder in the manner of one who believed she was beautiful, desirable. Still in short skirts, tops with plunging necklines, still with painted face and fluttering eyelashes — a caricature of her young self. Dropping my burning eyes, I lifted my hands to my hot cheeks and felt wetness on them.

CHAPTER THIRTY

While still paralyzed in the middle of the room, I heard a cry. Turning, I saw Louisa stumble, glimpsed a platform shoe fall from her foot. I got to her first, helped her into a chair, and retrieved the shoe.

"Listen," I whispered urgently in her ear, "I've come to say something to you. It's important. You have to listen — no, please stay. Please listen to me. I *must* tell you!"

Thick pink lips drew themselves into another pout. Frown lines were carved deeply into her forehead, and beneath it, heavily blackened eyelashes fluttered. She raised one hand to flick her wayward hair, and with the other, arranged her skirt in such a way that the slit was in front.

Even now she couldn't help herself. Even at her age she had to seduce — or try to seduce — every male she encountered. Even me! And a bottomless misery for her, for both of us, swept over me. To her, I was only a faded memory, someone inconsequential. She'd only been attracted to me and stuck with me because I was the one man among a universe of others who hadn't been easy to conquer. How quickly that attraction had passed when greener pastures were everywhere, were more readily available, more exciting than anything my virginal self could offer. I was an anomaly, a mystery to be solved, just one more difficult fellow to conquer.

"I told you I didn't love you, that I hated you," I blurted, desperate now to get the words out. But already she was looking away, so my words spouted out of my mouth quickly, frantically.

"I didn't mean it," I said again. "I loved you, loved you more than anybody, more than anything else in the world. You were the whole wide universe to me, and I only said what I did because I could never give you children … and … and because I knew you wanted them …"

She didn't appear to have been listening but must have been, because at the word *children*, she trained puzzled eyes on me.

"*Children?* What do they have to do with anything? I never wanted any. I only said I did to please you …" Vague curiosity entered her eyes. "Why don't you sit here? I'll get you another beer. Molson, I suppose? You can wait until I finish my shift at eight. Then you can tell me all your fairy tales." She rubbed her foot, put her shoe back on, got up, and hobbled to the bar.

Wounded beyond measure, I huddled in the corner of the pub, taking gulps of beer and casting furtive glances at her while she took orders, waited on tables, and when not busy, propped her elbows on the counter and stared into space.

Why was I here — for her? For myself? Did the past even matter anymore? She didn't seem to remember it, or if she did, she didn't care.

Finally, at fifteen minutes after eight, Louisa beckoned for me to follow her, and we climbed the stairs to the main floor and out into the night. Numbly, I trailed her across Spadina Avenue and into a sprawling old house on the other side, through ramshackle rooms running off a central hallway, and into one at the back. She lived in a single room in a student rooming house!

Illuminated by street lights just outside the big bay window, I saw a large room, mahogany-panelled and once elegant.

Neat, spartan, I thought as I let my eyes range over the few furnishings, over a tidy stack of paperbacks and magazines on a bookshelf along one wall. The only decorative objects were a porcelain figurine and a framed family photograph on the chimney mantel. Dominating the room was a double bed covered with a red bedspread of some shiny material, and a large empty fireplace.

"Okay, so this is my place," Louisa said without preamble. "Sit down somewhere. Of course, I remember you, but that was a long time ago, and I'm not sure what you want with me after all this time, do I? You said something about children, but what has that to do with anything? I don't know what you want, do I?"

She turned on a lamp, and in its light, I saw that her eyes were bloodshot, she looked tired, the lines about her eyes deeper than I'd noticed in the dim light of the pub. Maybe she drank too much.

"Do you live here alone?" I asked.

She shrugged. "Why? You want to keep me company, sleep with me?" Leaning against the mantel, she stared at her hands and picked at her fingernails for so long that I wondered if she'd forgotten I was there.

"Louisa!" I cried. "For heaven's sake, we were going to get married —"

"And you changed your mind, didn't you?" She looked up without interest, her tone indifferent. "So? As I said before, what do you want now?"

"It wasn't that I changed my mind." I bent forward in my chair, my voice urgent. "I loved you ... *loved* you! I only told you I never did so you'd go away because ... because I couldn't give you children. And you wanted them. I thought you would pretend you didn't, but that later you might change your mind. Then you'd come to hate me."

"You said all that before." Sudden amusement entered

her voice as she added, "*I* wanted children? I hate the little bastards, don't I? I never wanted to have any, like never." Now her eyes focused sharply on me, taking in my clothes — smart casual — my receding hairline, the whole six-foot bulk of me, as though sizing up a potential date.

She smiled and straightened. "How big and quaint you are. You always were an odd one. Really, Julian, why would I want kids when I grew up among six of them? I hated it, didn't I? The mess, the noise, the crowding and stealing of my clothes, my underpants, my shirts — everything. Whenever I needed something, one of my sisters had already taken it and nobody cared whatsoever. I was going to have my own place, wasn't I? Neat and tidy and everything in its place and nobody else to touch it. I thought you would be okay to live with because you were careful, thoughtful — a bit dull, mind you — but you would've done." She moved from the mantel to the bay window and pulled a curtain across it. When she turned back to me, she became more animated than she'd been so far.

"God, now you come to tell me, what, almost forty years later, that you're sorry? I suppose you think you want to marry me, now that we're too old to have children." She laughed in her usual way, but the sound of it now grated.

"You mean you didn't really care that I did that to you? You just went on to somebody else? Did you get married, after all, and have children?"

"Children? Why do you keep going on about them? I already told you. For heaven's sake, why would I want children? I hated them. What I wanted was order, to know where things were, that my things were my own. I told you that when I went to put on my shoes, they were gone. Socks — I never had any that matched. My sisters said I should be glad to share. Share! But I had nothing to share. I was never going to have kids and live like that! You've got no idea. You dreamed about big families and thought all the joy in the world was to be found in having brothers and sisters, but it was a mess, it was chaos, it's ... you saw how it was." She walked back to the mantel and propped an elbow on it, cupping her head in one hand.

I searched my memory, trying to recall when I'd told Mom we were getting married and would have a whole pile of kids. I remembered it now: Louisa's voice, when she spoke, had been flat. She'd said something like: "If that's what you want, Julian, of course I do, too."

"Did you get married?" I asked suddenly.

"Married!" she spat. "How can anyone promise to love someone for the rest of their life? People get carried away by that bullshit!"

I would have loved her for the rest of my life. Or would I have? At that moment, with Louisa a few feet from me, I wondered for the first time what exactly it was I'd felt for her. Love? Infatuation? A form of obsession? Would she have grown and developed differently if we'd been together? It seemed to me now that she was stuck in the early 1970s, saw herself still as a teenager.

Startled out of my thoughts by a brush of hair across my face, I glanced up to find Louisa leaning over me, fluffing her hair about her face. She lifted a hand, raised my chin, and peered into my eyes. The same old come-hither look was back in hers.

"I see you're a man of some means," she said in the sing-song voice I remembered. "You look like you've done well, Julian. Are *you* married? If you are, you must have come looking for something you don't get from your wife. You came back to your old flame thinking you can get whatever it is from her. That's what you thought, isn't it? Here's some news for you. You'll have to pay for it, pay for what I would've given you for free back then. But you didn't want it, only once that I remember."

Her last words were spoken with bitterness.

"You've got it all wrong," I said, raising my voice. "I came to tell you how sorry I am and explain why I said I didn't love you back then, to find out if you had children. Did you have any?"

"The damn children thing again. Did I have kids? I had one, accidentally, and I never wanted her."

I was shocked. "I hope she didn't know that. Where is she now?"

"How should I know? She left home, didn't she? Look, what do you want from me? I don't care about what you did or didn't do back then. It's gone and done and who cares anymore? You want to have me now?"

I recoiled. Suddenly, I loathed myself, my naivety. I was indeed as she'd said — a quaint one. Oddball, some would say. Louisa was a pub waitress and part-time prostitute. I was merely a man of some means she'd use to get what she could out of me. I meant nothing else to her, only an out-of-date memory.

Never had an idol crashed so far, so fast. My infatuation, my obsession, or whatever it was or had been, lifted, or rather, was violently smashed. My mind reeled and I thought I would be sick. I recalled the burden of guilt and the sense of obligation I'd carried around for decades. Like murderers, convicts, or thieves, I'd felt the need to confess, to find out I hadn't wrecked another person's life and so ease my obsession. Or was there something else, as Louisa had suggested, that I was looking for that was missing in my own life. In my wife?

My wife. In that austere room devoid of the clutter of any ordinary person's life, I summoned Penny's face. It came to me clearly, beautiful, clean, and unambiguous. Everything about her told me who she was, that what she felt for me would never change. I knew then that everything else was up to me.

When I finally left Louisa's flat, it was with relief mixed with a certain degree of emptiness, and strangely enough, gladness. Before returning to Mom and Dad's, I drove slowly past Uncle Albert's old apartment on St. Clair, conjuring up comforting images of him. Proceeding north on Yonge Street, I caught sight of a familiar figure about to enter Yorkminster Park Baptist Church on the corner of Heath Street. I recognized Steve. *But going into a church?* In the aftermath of my encounter with Louisa, I felt flat, empty. I had nothing within me to engage with him.

I left Toronto on a dull, hazy day, the clouds lowered and the city skyline indistinct. I was bruised, drained, but relieved.

The air cleared as we flew west, the Rockies on the Alberta-B.C. border rising sharply, white and icy. Vancouver, as we descended, was bathed in clean sunlight.

CHAPTER THIRTY-ONE

After landing at the Vancouver airport, I raced home to our condo and flew in the door, arms outstretched and a huge smile on my face. Penny stood in the doorway, waiting to learn what I would say, what I would do. At the sight of me, a huge idiotic grin on my face rushing to her, her own face softened, and it struck me that she was beautiful, really beautiful. She was uncomplicated, straightforward. My relief was so overwhelming that I grabbed her, hugged her thin frame so tightly that she cried out, "Hey, Jules, you're suffocating me!"

"I love you. Do you know that?" And I began laughing until Penny's smiling face changed and frown lines creased her face.

"You owe me," she said.

"What?"

"An explanation."

Penny, the solid one of the two of us, the tree trunk, the branches that remained true, that could withstand wind and rain and hurricanes, now wanted something else.

And so I made a true confession.

She remained quiet, listening intently, but said little. We moved around each other carefully and formally, and still she said nothing. Only at the dinner table the next day did she look straight at me and ask, "Okay, any more secrets?"

I hesitated as Steve came to mind, Steve deprived of an

inheritance in favour of me, in effect now trying to blackmail me. But he had nothing to hold over me, and I could talk to him some other time about money.

"No!" I said emphatically, and she believed me.

That weekend we resumed our old routines. I sat at the piano — Uncle Albert's — and played the sonatas and symphonies Penny most loved. I renewed my love affair with the view from our condo: Burrard Inlet, the spreading sea, the sharp, snowy North Shore Mountains, and with the quiet world outside our door. I supposed my life would unfold and I'd trek on in just such a predictable manner.

Until the phone rang.

Penny picked it up. "For you, from the office." Her brows lifted in surprised inquiry.

"Julian." At Ian's brusque voice, harsh colours flew through the air. "I know you've only been home a short while, but you're to be in the office tomorrow first thing!"

I fell back into my chair. Either I was going to be given a chance to redeem myself or be fired.

The next morning, Ian stood above my desk, looking at me but not smiling. "We've got a new client. I'm putting you in charge of it. Are you up to it?" His voice was cold.

Are you up to it? I remembered Uncle Albert's words from long ago.

"Yes, siree!" I answered as I'd done as a boy back then. Ian smiled slightly and gave me a thumbs-up.

That wasn't all.

One day, several weeks after my trip to Toronto, a young woman knocked on our condo door just after I returned from work, having redeemed myself there. Penny answered, and a thirty-something woman stood in the doorway, her head almost reaching the top. Ill at ease, her broad face flamed crimson with embarrassment, in halting words she said she was Claire Blackstock.

The name meant nothing to Penny, who stood gaping at her. "Julian, you better come here. You better talk to this girl."

I sauntered in from the spare bedroom that I used for a study and into the living room. After taking one look at the girl, I thought I'd pass out. "Dear Lord Almighty!" I cried as I stared at her. She was tall, and like me, had protruding ears, a square jaw, a wide forehead, and a full head of light brown hair. Her initial blush of colour faded, leaving her with a dull, patchy pallor. She was skeletally thin, her cheeks hollow. And her eyes, when she raised them briefly, were the same blue-grey as mine, but sunk deep into their sockets.

Blackstock? That was Louisa's maiden name.

"Did you know … how … what do you know of me? How did you find me?"

After a prolonged silence, she replied haltingly, "Your cousin, Steve. He gave me your address. He said you'd look after me. He said … he said … you're my father." She folded her hands in front of her, eyes remaining on the floor.

A daughter? I dropped into the chair nearest me, my mouth open but nothing coming out of it. Penny stood rigidly in front of the girl, hands twitching at her sides. I glanced up at my wife. Deep lines furrowed her brow, and she curled and uncurled her fingers in the palms of her hands. Her mouth opened and closed. Then, with restless movements, she strode around the living room, to the windows and back again, to peer at the girl called Claire. When eventually she found her voice, she said briskly, "You'd better sit down and talk to us."

A daughter! And Steve: what did he intend?

Penny made tea, put out a plate of biscuits and a lump of cheese, then sat straight-backed on a dining room chair, swivelling her eyes between Claire and me. "This is very awkward for us — for Julian," she said with no inflection in her voice. "Julian can't … could never have children, so how can it be that you're his daughter?" The girl stared at her lap, her tea untouched. After watching her for a few moments, Penny added, "But I must say there's quite a resemblance."

At those words I shook myself out of my trance and gazed hard at Claire. What I saw was my younger self, only feminized, and I knew instantly she had to be my daughter. The likeness was too striking. She must have been conceived the one and only time Louisa and I had slept together, and again I heard Louisa's voice: *A girl never gets pregnant the first time with a guy.*

This was the daughter Louisa had given birth to, that she hadn't bothered to tell me about and obviously didn't care about whatsoever. What was Steve's motivation in sending her to me? I saw again the shifting eyes in the square face, the neck that sat crunched on his shoulders. After a lifetime of booze and drugs, maybe he'd gone to church and found God — and my daughter! Hadn't I seen him enter a church at Yonge and Heath? I couldn't adequately begin to describe my emotions. All I knew was that a rainbow of colours flitted around the room, among them streaks of purple and scarlet mixed with soft yellows. Fury toward Louisa raged hotly through me, along with guilt, shame, and regret. Then came elation. Euphoria. A sense of confusion mixed with guilt on Penny's behalf.

Penny, in her matter-of-fact way, after searching my face, told Claire she could stay, and these were the rules: truthfulness at all times. Punctuality for meals and for coming in at night. Tidiness. Assistance with household chores. And getting professional help.

"Is that all you have with you?" Penny asked, pointing at the small knapsack Claire had dropped on the floor beside her chair.

Claire just nodded without raising her head. Her face had faded to greyish-white. I noticed her fingernails were bitten to the quick, that she swayed slightly in her chair. Wrapping her thin arms around herself, she hunched lower, as if wishing to become invisible.

"Claire, where have you been living up until now?" I asked.

Without looking at me, in a monotone, she replied, "Here and there." She paused, then added, "Your cousin, Steve, I met him … he took me to the Baptist church at Yonge and Heath. He told me about you, where you lived, that you'd help me. He said it's for God to forgive, to tell you that, and you'd understand."

I felt as if I'd swallowed the universe, its sweetness as well as its poison. I had no idea what to do with my emotions: wild elation followed fury … and profound pity. Then came particular anger toward Louisa, who hadn't cared, who had abandoned every responsibility belonging to a parent.

I glanced at Penny. She looked at me. Moments passed.

Penny got to her feet. "Jules," she said while looking at Claire, "I'll move a few of your things, open up the couch in your study for a bed, and make it into a bedroom for Claire. Okay?"

"Thank you, Penny," I whispered.

Penny disappeared. Claire remained huddled in the armchair near the fireplace without speaking, and still stunned, still not believing this was real, I felt my mind suddenly race. Mom and Dad had a granddaughter! I had a daughter! I'd believed in something all my life that wasn't true. I'd lived a lie. I'd given up Louisa for this lie.

Louisa. My thoughts of her blackened, and I really, truly, came to hate her on behalf of Claire and what she'd done to the girl — the obvious neglect, the emotional abuse.

∞

"What made you think you were sterile?" Penny asked me after Claire had gone to bed that night. "What I mean is, did you never actually sleep with any girl before ... before me? And if you did, did you practise birth control?"

"No. Louisa was the only girl I ever slept with." My voice was humble, and I wondered if I should have been proud of this fact or ashamed. "Penny, I don't know what to say or think. A daughter ..."

"You always wanted kids, didn't you?"

"Of course!"

"Well, then, now you have one, Jules. You'll be a father, but it won't be easy. It looks to me like she's got an eating disorder, and I hope to God not, but an addiction problem, too."

"You're saying drugs?"

"Don't be naive, Jules. You saw her. Look, I'm willing to have her live with us while she gets herself sorted out, if that's what you want."

"You mean, you're willing to be a mother to her?" I could hardly breathe.

"Well, I wouldn't go that far, but we can certainly look after her for a while and try to help her."

A rush of giddy sensations hit me. A confusion of colours, like strobe lights, fell over me, and I couldn't wait to tell Mom and Dad, especially Mom, who would be ecstatic. I got up, and at that moment dark clouds parted, allowing the last rays of the sun to filter through the westward-facing windows. In the now yellow-spangled room, I strode to the piano, lifted the lid, and struck the F major chord, a clean, pure, unambiguous sound. I laughed as it echoed around the room.

Later came thoughts about Steve, about what I owed him, and not just money.

When I did pick up the phone to call my parents, Uncle Robert answered. I asked for Mom, and because she wasn't home, because I was so pumped with the need to tell someone, I said, "Tell my mom she's got a granddaughter. Tell her to call me."

"So you spawned a kid, after all. I suppose miracles do happen. Congrats." After a pause, he asked, "Do you know whose son *you* are?"

"I … what?"

He laughed. "Ask your mother." Then he hung up.

∞

I could tell Mom was crying when she confessed toa me that I was Uncle Albert and Aunt Clarissa's son. "Your uncle, when Aunt Clarissa died, he couldn't look after you and he knew how desperately your dad and I wanted a child — you know how much. So we raised you as our own. But, Julian, you know how much your Uncle Albert loved you. You saw how he acted as a father to you."

When Penny came home that late afternoon, I was weeping in our bedroom, crying for Uncle Albert and how I could have been more of a real son to him if I'd known. For my mother, my father, for my daughter, Claire. For my whole life that might have been with Louisa, and how lucky for me it wasn't.

ACKNOWLEDGEMENTS

My thanks to Michael Carroll, my editor and my supporter, without whom this book might never have arrived. Thank you also to my readers, including Helen Taylor-Allan, Pat Vickers, Anita Taylor, Sarah Mayor, and Bernice Lever.